Hands-On Homicide

Sarah Hualde

Cover by GetCovers.com

Edited by Mikayla Ruth

For Steveo

Chapter 1

Spa Life

I drowned in a serenity pond. Well, almost. Peaceful music, slow-flowing water, and a murderous attack. The irony sang to me as I blacked out, watching a rose gold earbud drift in the current of my last air bubble.

Hours before, my shift at Hands On Healing Spa waxed on as normal. Davis Pile, a fellow masseuse, helped his latest client, an older lady, out to her car. A summer rain thrummed outside the glass doors. He used his raincoat to shield her from the sudden storm.

Mr. Tucker Williams, my current client, rolled his shoulders with ease as he paid his bill. "Corky, you're amazing. How do you know exactly where to work?"

I shrugged. I didn't know how I knew. I just did. Tucker walked into his appointment with his shoulders rolled in toward his clavicle, a sure sign of tight pectoral muscles. The underlying causes were a broken heart, acute anxiety, and or deep sadness. My bodywork could only give him so much relief. Instead, Mr. Williams needed to confront his feelings with gentle understanding. However, I wasn't about to tell the macho cowboy to round up his trapped emotions.

Instead, I said, "Lots of training. I'm glad it was helpful."

"Helpful?" Tucker scoffed.

Massage therapy was a passion of mine, and I never stopped training. "Miracle worker," Tucker said to the receptionist and pointed his thumb in my direction.

Melinda Carlie frowned as always when Mr. Williams turned his gaze. She strongly despised the moments when I received compliments. In fact, she despised everything about me. Much like Tucker Williams's trapped trauma, my Melinda problems rested just above my breastbone.

"Y'all don't pay her enough," Mr. Williams said with a wink and a smile.

"We're so glad you're satisfied," Melinda said, disgust rising in her tone. "Shall we schedule your next visit?"

The front door chimed before Tucker could respond, bringing in Mrs. Valerie

Hewitt and Miss Emma Woods. The first was a regular client of mine, and the second came once a week for one of Stella Michael's famous facial treatments.

Stella was my best friend and had been since junior high. Miss Woods and Mrs. Hewitt chatted amongst themselves as Davis Pile joined the queue behind Mr. Williams.

Mrs. Hewitt waited beside the counter as Mr. Williams paid Melinda. She grinned at me and motioned me over to her side. I kept one eye on my last client while I made my way to her. I figured Mr. Williams was giving me his usual tip. I hoped that he doesn't give it to Melinda because if so, I'd never see a dime.

"You're early," I said, checking the wall clock. "I thought our appointment was in an hour."

"It is dear," Mrs. Hewitt said. "I have something important to attend to at work, and it can't wait. Could Henry take my spot instead?" Henry was Mr. Hewitt.

I didn't bother to ask what was so pressing that she'd give up her hot stone massage. Mrs. and Mr. Hewitt were therapists, so they couldn't tell me if it was work related. If the stress knot resting on Mrs. Hewitt's shoulders meant anything-it was.

"I don't see why that couldn't work," I said. "We'll get Melinda to schedule it." I waved to Melinda, who pocketed my well-deserved tip right before my eyes. She blinked and withdrew one bill, setting it down before me. "Thanks," I said. "But..."

Melinda turned back to Mr. Williams, who'd missed the transaction between Melinda, as she preferred being called, and me while he signed his credit card receipt. I frowned as Mel ignored me. Stella strolled up and winked in my direction before escorting Miss Woods away.

"Can you handle Melinda?" Mrs. Hewitt asked. She checked her watch. "I really have to go."

"You've got it," I said. "Don't wait too long to reschedule."

"Then I can finally get this kink out of my neck." Her hand flew to the offending tensed muscle. "Thanks, Corky," she said as she walked out, followed by the handsome Mr. Williams.

Melinda scowled at me before pivoting toward the back room. "Mr. and Mrs. Hewitt are switching places," I told her as she retreated. She hardly flinched.

I grumbled around the desk and found the Hewitts's entries. Correcting them was a cinch. Still, Mel would spit venom if she caught me messing with her perfect planner.

I returned to the treatment rooms to help Davis organize his area for his next client. One thing I knew for certain was that later Stella and I would have a Melinda venting session.

"Is Melinda always like that to you?" Davis asked as the table blankets billowed into place. I loaded the towel warmer as I answered.

"Pretty much. I try to ignore it."

Davis grunted and slid the headrest into place. "I wouldn't ignore it if I were you. Bullies don't stop because we look the other way. They have to be put in their place."

I glanced up at the very serious masseuse. "I'm not sure it's worth the effort."

"They bullied me badly in high school. Made my life a nightmare. But I got even." Davis winked playfully after his foreboding comment.

I smiled. "Did you spit in someone's root beer?"

Davis laughed. "Something like that."

I pushed play on the ambient music and stepped away from the spa. "Did it work?"

Davis waved a hand in the air and snapped his fingers. "Never bothered me again."

I cradled the soiled sheets in my hand. "Maybe I'll have to try it," I said as Davis met me in the hall. He turned toward reception.

"You won't regret it," he said. "And I'll have your back."

I chuckled. Davis was new in town but already a friendly addition to the spa. His banter with me and Stella drove Mel crazy. The perk made every shift breeze by.

At last afternoon ticked into the evening, and the day wrapped to a close. Stella Michaels knocked on the door to my therapy room. Her big brown eyes cast the snarky attitude that made her one of my favorite people. "Hey, Corky," Stella said. "Guess who's signing in?"

I placed my hands on my hips and took in the spotless room, which was all prepped for the weekend without me. It was a weekend I hoped would come early. Hands-On Healing, the spa I worked for, held to a strict grace period. Ten minutes past the hour, the spa canceled the client's appointment, charged their credit card, and handed the therapist a short reprieve from duty. Mr. Hewitt was thirty minutes behind schedule.

"No," I whined. "She didn't."

Stella clicked her spearmint gum against her molars. "Melinda's sending him back as soon as he pays."

"Pays beforehand?"

My best friend's eyebrow peaked in disdain. "Yup," she said, knowing that Melinda not only shoved my weekend farther back but stiffed my tip. Again! I was livid.

Stella continued. "Miss Woods will be in the quiet room, after her next treatment. Honestly, I don't know why she bothers with the quiet room. She's always plugged into one of her lonely-hearts podcasts. I think she has at least one earbud docked in place. Even during her treatments. It's insulting." Stella crossed her arms. Her final facial of the day was finished. She was as ready for Friday as I was.

"Good thing she's nice." I retorted, defending the town's most popular high school counselor and teacher.

Stella rolled her eyes. "Good thing she let me ace Government."

Stella nearly repeated twelfth grade because of her year of teen angst. She hosted a grin of nostalgia. Miss Woods was a young soul and coached Stella instead of allowing her to flunk. "Mr. Hewitt is the last massage of the day. Melinda's logging him in, and then she's leaving."

"Meanwhile, I get to treat Mr. Hewitt past closing, clean, and lock up," I groaned.

"Yup," Stella snapped her gum once more. "You get to do your job and hers, and I get to hit up the grocery store, while she starts her weekend early with Brett Booker."

My skin chilled after hearing my ex's name. Bad history didn't describe my past with Brett and Melinda. Our past tracked back into high school. I shuddered, striving to shake off the coldness from the thought.

Melinda loved to prod me with every hot poker she could find. No doubt she'd walk Mr. Hewitt to the room and use her saccharin front desk voice to explain Mr. Hewitt's lateness and my assumed happiness to accommodate him. I could sense her snotty smile before I heard her heels clip down the hall.

Stella winked at me. "I'll bring you coffee."

"No sugar," I added.

"Of course," Stella added as she shot finger guns at me. "Besides, Steve's planned a whole tapas theme meal. He wouldn't want to waste your carbs on simple syrup."

"Sounds awesome," I said, with excitement in my voice. I was thrilled that Stella's brother enjoyed studying for his culinary class by spoiling us.

"Don't rush," Stella added. "Dinner isn't until eight. We've got time to decompress before Chef Steve gets frantic."

I smiled as Stella "accidentally" knocked into Melinda while she and Mr. Hewitt swung into view, proving my hypothesis.

I stood face-to-face with Melinda, leaving my client to get comfy on the table. She snarled. "Your friend doesn't have to be such a twerp."

"You know her name," I pointed out.

According to Melinda, everything was my fault, and she enjoyed blaming me. Sure, Stella was my bestie, but she was also Melinda's coworker and fellow alumni of Deadhorse Canyon High.

Melinda ignored me. "Did she tell you I'm leaving?"

"Forever?" I whispered. If Melinda caught my dig, she pretended I hadn't spoken.

"I'm tidying up the front desk," She continued. "I would appreciate it if you and Stella kept your hands off the schedule." I assumed she meant me penciling Mr. Hewitt into Mrs. Hewitt's place. As if erasing an S was going to ruin her precious system. "I was trying to sign in a new client today, which was embarrassing. As if scribbling over names isn't unprofessional enough. You can't tear out pages whenever you feel like it."

I didn't know what she was griping about and didn't care to find out. I loved my job, even if it meant late clients and braving a passive-aggressive receptionist. When my client knocked on the wall, I counted to ten and gladly ditched Melinda in the hallway.

Chapter 2

Into the Quiet

Working on Mr. Hewitt was a breeze compared to Melinda's drama. My fingers knew where to focus the instant they brushed his skin. Unlike most of my clients, financial problems never knotted his hips. Instead, grief and sadness nestled on his pecs and neck. Carrying the weight of his clients was the cause, or so I guessed.

After the basics with some trigger point therapy, I settled a warm towel on Mr. Hewitt's shoulders and played some calming music. I'd put away his personal essential oil mix when he had been late, and I had forgotten to remake it before his bodywork.

"I'll be back in three minutes with your special blend," I whispered. Mr. Hewitt offered a sleepy grunt in response as I shut the door calmly behind me.

The burbling of the Serenity Pond drew my attention. Stella must've left it going. I slid into the stockroom and gathered my supplies. Mr. Hewitt's relaxation blend was made up of grapeseed oil, eucalyptus, lavender, and spearmint.

I poured Mr. Hewitt's mix into an amber bottle, enjoying the aroma. I imagined being a therapist wasn't a simple job, but working with a spouse, also a therapist, probably amplified the anxiety. No wonder the couple paid for weekly massages. I listened to their muscles and energy while they drooled on my table. If I ever needed the services of a paid confidant, I would choose one of the Hewitts to help me.

I tucked the essential oil bottles away in their places and spotted neon pink sticky notes adorned with Melinda's loopy cursive. "Corky, don't forget to squeegee the showers." She completed the memo with a passive-aggressive smiling face.

"Punk," I whispered.

Cleaning was Melinda's job, not mine. It was just one more responsibility she'd left for me. I ripped the note from the cupboard and tossed it into the trash bin, noting it hadn't been dumped. I growled and took a long inhale of Mr. Hewitt's oil. Mr. Hewitt didn't deserve my frustration, even if he held up my weekend.

For Mr. Hewitt's final rubdown, I focused on his neck and shoulders. He sat chatting on the edge of my table in a plush robe. "It's been a terrible week," he said.

"I guessed as much," I replied, holding my thumb under a sore spot under his occipital bone. Mr. Hewitt sighed as it was released.

"You do a kind thing and..." Mr. Hewitt trailed off. "Maybe that's the problem."

"Kindness?" I asked, only half-listening. I trailed my thumbs along the ridge of his shoulder blades, encouraging another knot to unravel.

He laughed. "Volunteer work comes with bonus problems."

Everyone knew the Hewitts for their generosity. Since they spent their free afternoons working at the senior center or youth home, I assumed they had more free cases than paying clients. Maybe Mr. Hewitt was referring to one such case.

"We all know you don't take on pro-Bono cases for the fun of it," I stated as one last tension ball rolled away from Mr. Hewitt's shoulder.

Mr. Hewitt groaned. "Sometimes, I wish I cared more about the money than the people."

That was a laugh, I thought. "Don't we all," I answered with sarcasm in my voice.

Mr. Hewitt chuckled low. "Do you need to talk?" I asked.

"I wish I could," he said. "Just hurting people, hurting people."

"Hurting you?" I asked.

"Not directly," he answered as I finished the final round of tapotement.

"I'm sorry about that," I said, meaning it. "I wish I could help. At least you're not a stiff bundle of knots anymore. You're all done."

"Once again, Corky Hobbs, you've worked wonders." Mr. Hewitt slowly rolled his neck from side to side. He didn't have that much movement before lying on my table.

"Just doing my job," I smirked.

"It's more than that," he sighed. "You see inside of people, and Valerie agrees with me."

I turned away, hiding my wide smile at the compliment from the Hewitts.

My phone vibrated across the front desk as I waved goodbye to Mr. Hewitt. Rushing to answer what I thought was

Stella, I stumbled on my feet and smacked into one of the spa's potted ferns. Soil spewed across the floor toward the showers, reminding me I needed to clean it, too.

I crawled to the front desk and responded to Stella's message. She saved me, telling me Iced Java was on its way.

I gave Stella a thumbs-up before returning to my chores. The front door chimed as I retrieved the broom and dustbin.

"You're speedy," I called out to Stella. She didn't reply.

Stella busied herself in the quiet room as I swept up my spill. I heard her cleaning. "Bless your heart," I said, thrilled she'd come back to help me close.

Neither of us got paid to do Melinda's job, but working together would ease the load. I entered the small dark lounge. The overhead lights of the quiet room stayed off during working hours, but I was used to working in low lights. I hurried across the tiles to the shower and locker room. I scrubbed the glass doors of the showers dreaming of the cold coffee awaiting me. Knowing I was alone in a nearly soundproof space gave me the jitters. Goosebumps bristled on my arm even before a sudden draft of cold brushed across my skin.

The hair prickled on the back of my neck. Was someone behind me? I spun."Stells Bells? Are you here?" A low moan answered me. Followed by a splash. I snorted. "Clumsy goof! You better not drop my coffee!"

Snatching a towel, I charged into the room of relaxation, intending to mock my friend's attempt to spook me. But Stella wasn't there. Neither was my blended dark chocolate, sugar-free coffee.

A shuffling sound startled me. I stepped toward the fountain, using its ambient light to get a better look.

Crunch! My knees buckled as my head cracked. The towel slipped from my hand. Then I was wet. Bubbles tangled around my hair. Scented water soaked into my shirt as a pair of hands held my neck beneath the water. I commanded my arms to fight and my body to flail. The message didn't relay to my limbs. A tiny rose gold earbud coasted past me as if it were chilling at a water park.

A truck backfired in the parking lot. Was that Stella's truck? Who would have been in the quiet room if it wasn't Stella? I opened my mouth to call out to her, swallowing a mouthful of water. The hands holding my head slammed my face against the bottom of the fountain. Then I drifted off to sleep.

Chapter 3

Double Ouch

"Ouch," I mumbled.

"Corky?" Steve Michaels hustled to my side.

"Get a nurse," Stella ordered.

My temples throbbed while I squinted against the overhead lighting. Shoes squeaked along the tile floor, then returned, bringing another set.

Cold, firm hands wrapped around my wrist—a searing flash stabbed at my head, and flickering moments rolled through my mind.

"I thought she was a goner," a woman whispered.

"What?" I asked. There was a sandpaper edge in my voice.

"What?" the whispering stranger echoed.

I blinked, still fighting against the fluorescents. "Why is it so bright in here?"

"I'll get the light," Steve's voice said.

The sunlight grew dimmer, allowing me to crack my eyes open. "I feel like I've been swimming without my goggles."

Stella's laugh drew my attention, and she hurried to my side. Her short, dark hair bounced as she approached. "Corky, you had us so scared." Stella bent and kissed my forehead.

"Do you know where you are?" The whisperer asked.

I saw Steve lean against the hospital wall by the door.

"The hospital?"

"Good guess," she said.

I turned to face a nurse sporting cartoon character scrubs. She inspected my eyes, and then the IV in my arm. She gently touched my skin with her bare hand. She whispered again. "I thought the cravings were supposed to subside after three days. Instead, whenever I get a menthol hit, my fingers tremble."

"Sorry, it's probably me," I said.

The nurse glared in curiosity back at me. "What's you?"

"Making you crave a cigarette," I answered. "Mr. Hewitt's oil has mint in it."

"What?" The nurse tossed glances at me and then my friends.

"I don't understand. What does that have to do with having a cigarette?" Stella asked.

"Does your friend smoke?" The nurse turned toward Stella.

"Nope, never has."

I raised my free hand to my face and sniffed. I smelled soap, rubbing alcohol, and Stella's favorite avocado body butter. No aromatherapy lingered.

The nurse squinted and looked into my face. She put her hand on my forehead. "I think your friend is confused. That's typical." She turned toward Stella and Steve. The nurse walked away taking her backstory with her. Stella explained my parents had stepped out to get everyone dinner.

Steve approached the hospital bed. "You okay?" He asked in his shy, deep voice.

I nodded. Ouch! Instant regret.

"Your head?"

"You guessed it," I answered, smacking my lips. "And I'm thirsty. I don't suppose Stella brought my coffee along."

Stella returned to my bedside. "Coffee? Corks, that was yesterday."

"Yesterday?" My head swirled around Stella's revelation as the cartoon-clad nurse clogged back toward me. That's when I remembered strawberry blond hair waving in the water beside me.

I sank back onto my pillow. Mom would be back any minute. I needed rest before her onslaught of concern overran the room. Too late.

"Sweet baby," she cooed as she rushed to my bed.

After long bouts of talking and crying, Mom and Dad returned home to prepare the house for me. Whatever that meant. I figured Dad was probably calling the church prayer tree to give a praise report. Mom would be remaking my bed, trying to make my home cozy and welcoming for recovery. I was exhausted when they left and, as a result, drifted off into a dreamless sleep.

The next morning, I was released back into the world. Bouncing along the pitted streets of Deadhorse Canyon, small-town USA, I held my head in my hands and stared out the window. Stella and her brother shared the backfiring blue truck. I expected Stella or my parents to come get me. Instead, Steve picked me up.

"Where's Stella and my parents?" I asked my driver.

"Waiting for you," Steve said. His face flickered with a sideways half-smile. This was Steve's look when he had a secret. He was holding something back. I stared at him and waited.

Steve's knuckles flexed on the wheel. He was a sweet guy who despised confrontation. He also had a hard time telling people no. His sister teased him about all his traits that I found endearing in a big brother sort of way.

"Come on, Corks," he mumbled, avoiding me. "Seven minutes until we're there. Can't you wait seven minutes?"

I shrugged. "If I must," I spouted before dangling my bare feet out the open window.

I was still stunned by Stella's no-show at my hospital release. Usually, she's as much in my business as I am in hers.

Steve's phone pinged on the seat between us. "That must be her," Steve announced. "Go ahead, read it."

I quickly snatched his phone. "Are you sure? It may be your super-secret girlfriend," I teased. "I might just have to tell her you belong to me." Steve's cheeks pinked. He cleared his throat. "Easy." I nudged him with my elbow.

The brief brush of his arm against mine flashed memories of sitting together at graduation. His deep brown eyes looked into mine. I blinked, and the memory melted away. "You know I'm just teasing."

Steve chuckled.

I read the text. "She says it's all ready. What's ready?"

I scanned my attire. My favorite tank top, ratty and faded, and a pair of old gym shorts, looked ready for a sleep over with Stella but not a surprise party. I pulled up my visor to take a gander at my make-up-less face. The chief attraction was a nasty bruise on the left side of my head. It was turning from deep blue to green. "I'm a mess," I relented.

Steve glanced at me before setting his firm attention on the street. "You look fine."

"You're just being nice."

Stella stood in the driveway and held a bundle of balloons. I cringed. Balloons gave me the willies. Unexpected pops threw me into fits. I hated the jump scare balloons delivered. Thankfully, Stella was toting them to the trash barrels.

Steve chortled. "Your parents hoped to have them all cleaned up before you arrived. Most are from spa clients and church people. That's why they sent me to get you."

I jumped when the sound of popping latex squeezed through the open truck window. I curled into Steve's shoulder.

He put his hands around my ears. Memories of him hiding with me in his family's coat closet rolled to my mind. The sounds of clowns shaping balloons into animals from a dozen years back echoed as Steve shielded me. A knock on the passenger door drew me back to the present.

Stella ripped my door open. "Killed them all," she reported. "I guess that wasn't a brilliant choice of a verb. Sorry."

I waved Stella's worry away and slid down from the truck seat. "Thanks for doing that," I said.

"Your parents are preparing a feast," Stella said as her arm linked to mine. She walked me to the back gate as pictures of us skipping to music class whizzed into my head. The feelings accompanying the remembrance faded as Stella dropped my arm and unlocked the gate to my parent's backyard.

Living in a small house behind my parent's home had many perks. It hid me away from the main street. I relished the privacy. It gave me pause and a place to think without distraction. Though the cul-de-sac was quiet, I enjoyed the added benefit of not having an exposed front door. No well-wishers or solicitors could disturb me without unlocking or climbing the side gate, and very few people had the lock's passcode. Stella and Steve were two of my trusted gatekeepers, and I was proud to have them.

Steve's hand fell from my upper back and brushed my elbow as he turned to double-check the lock. The tenderness in his touch sent me back to the bleachers and his deep, chocolate eyes looking back into mine.

"Hold this," Stella snapped, shoving the bag into Steve's hands and breaking our brief connection. She fished through my purse and pulled out my house key.

Steve cocked his head as if checking me for defects. I raised a hand to my head and blinked at him. What just happened?

Stella guided me into my one-bedroom cottage and over to my sofa. "You went pale," she commented. "You need to rest."

I leaned against the back of my loveseat and tugged a well-worn family quilt over my legs. It wasn't cold out or chilly in my home, but I shivered.

"Just relax. I'll get you something to eat," Steve said as he opened my mini-fridge. He snorted and shook his head. Steve never approved of my less-than-delectable spread.

I'd released my chubby and unhappy self while in massage therapy school. My clothes were many sizes smaller than they'd been in high school, yet the whims of my chubby tastebuds were never far away. I protected my healthier self by keeping my food supplies to only basics. My fridge shelves hosted protein shakes and microwave diet meals. Steve despised my food choices, yet he never veered from his habit of inspecting my fridge.

Stella ignored her brother, like always. She sat beside me. Her almond eyes inspected me. "You look one spook short of a haunted house."

More shivers waved up my skin at her choice of words. I rubbed my arms. "Any news on my attacker?" I asked, without looking at my friend's worried expression.

Stella snuggled into her usual cross-legged position. Now that I was back on topic, she seemed satisfied I wouldn't faint. "And Miss Woods's murderer?"

I could feel the color drain from my skin and the nausea swirl in my stomach—much like Miss Woods's hair in the serenity pond.

Steve chastised. "That's not cool."

Stella snapped at her brother in self-defense. "There's no use in sheltering Corky."

I choked. "The question remains."

Stella shrugged. "Not that we've heard. I've been interviewed, and so have you. That's all I know for sure."

I countered. "Does that mean I'm a suspect?"

"If the killer did not attack you, you probably would be," my friend continued. "I've narrowed the search down."

"Stella, don't," Steve pulled out his sternest voice. "Give her a day."

I pulled my blanket higher. Stella reached out and grabbed my wrist.

"Don't you see?"

I didn't see it. Anything. First came the whisper. "I didn't mean to, not really," Stella said in a much younger voice. My friend tightened her grip.

As she did, memories attacked me relentlessly. Except these memories weren't my own. In my mind, I witnessed Stella flirt with Mr. Vos, her voice coach. A young fourteen-year-old crushed on her thirty-something tutor. Her mother's shadow graced the front room curtains as she chatted a wall away from lessons.

Unexpectedly, Mr. Vos's dark face returned Stella's flirtatiousness. Stella's sudden fear washed through me. I winced when Mr. Vos kissed her. Though I watched from above, the sensations were vivid. Shame and disappointment squashed her excitement and curiosity. I shook her hand from mine, and the feeling subsided.

Stella stared at me. "What happened?" She turned to Steve. "Grab her some water."

I took the bottle as Steve handed it over. Curling inside my blanket, I avoided another touch. What was going on?

"I've got to sleep," I said, standing on unsteady legs.

"Do you want me to walk you?" Stella asked as she rose from the seat.

"I'm okay. Will you be here when I wake up?"

Stella followed me halfway down the hall. "I'm not going anywhere."

"Good, because we have things to talk about," I said, tossing my tired mind and rattling body onto my messy bed.

"Yes, I can't wait to talk about the murder."

Stella's morbid enthusiasm worried me.

I frowned and said, "Not that. Mr. Vos." Stella's mouth dropped open just before I shut my eyes.

Chapter 4

Despite my Better Judgment

I awoke to the sound of intense weeping. The soul-churning kind of crying that only follows the death of someone or something precious. Worst of all, I knew the voice that mourned. It was my mother's.

I eavesdropped as she bellowed, wondering how I could hear her crying from my backyard cottage. That's when I noticed her sweet hand in mine. I sat straight up, ripping my hand away and startling my mom to bits. She howled before grabbing her chest and fanning herself back to stability.

"Dear Lord," she sputtered. "You nearly gave me a heart attack."

"I scared myself," I said as my head fluttered from its rapid ascent.

"What has you screaming like a banshee?" As soon as she asked, a penitent look replaced her scared expression. Her brown eyes softened behind her glasses. "Stupid of me to ask. I'm sorry. I'm sure you don't want to talk about the incident."

"The incident?" I asked dumbly, still not awake. That's when my memory flooded my glands, and the scent of eucalyptus and chlorine stung my nose. I knew the smell was a phantom, but that didn't mean my heart got the memo. It raced under my tank top and sent out panic responses to the rest of me, making me shiver once again.

Mom hurried to wrap my favorite blanket around me in her typical Mom fashion. She planted a kiss on my shoulder. What she meant as consolation sent my brain into a fit of sounds. In that second, the crying returned - louder and more pervasive than before.

"Could you not," I whispered. How was I supposed to ask my mom not to touch me? Touch was her primary love language. Some moms crafted gifts, some came to sports games, and others penned notes of affection to show how much they cared. My mother hugged the life out of anyone who needed it.

She pulled back slowly. A flicker of hurt marred her pretty face. "Oh, of course.

I should've known," she apologized, giving my heart a sting. "After a trauma, it's normal to need time. I can't imagine what you must be feeling." She reached out to touch me but pulled her hand away, remembering my request. Pain smeared her cheerful face.

It was too late. I forced myself free after seeing into her thoughts for a second.

"Normal." I hoped normal was still in the cards for me. At the moment, I felt anything but normal. As for trauma, another whiff of spa water scoured my memories of three nights back. There would be no return to normal for Miss Woods. Her burial was scheduled for Saturday.

After intense interviews and having dinner with both of my loving parents,

I dove back under my blankets, never wanting to resurface.

Denying them reassuring touches was impossible. Every slight contact turned me into an empathy magnet. The tapping of my hand sent visions of mom holding failed pregnancy tests. Every side hug from dad blurred with the guilt over his treatment of his little brother. I was thrilled to be back in my cottage.

I was used to sympathizing with others. At least in a small way. At work, I could feel what was lying beneath the surface of most of my clients. That didn't mean I watched them live out what clogged their flow and inflamed their joints. Sometimes I needed an extended break between clients, weary from their weariness but not experiencing their literal pain. What had me so suddenly intuitive? I didn't know, but I wanted it to stop.

I buried my head under my pillow, careful of my healing injury. The mattress rumbled as Stella flopped down beside me, assuming sister status. She made herself at home, burrowing her feet under my comfort quilt. I tried to ignore her presence, but my head throbbed. Stella's momentary silence worried me.

"Don't pretend like you're asleep. There's no way you're getting a rest until you spill," Stella scorned.

I flipped over, too exhausted to fight her. "Spill what?"

Stella frowned. "What's up with you? You're acting crazy."

Scoffing laughter blurted from my lips, making Stella's case for her. "Maybe this is what surviving a near-death experience looks like." I ran a flat hand beneath my chin to showcase my point.

"No," Stella said, piercing me with her scrutiny. "It's more than that."

"Do tell," I prodded, hoping my friend would lack the evidence necessary to continue her investigation.

When Stella held up her fist, ready to count off her proof, I knew it would be a long, long, long night.

She began detailing her observations. "First, you shudder whenever anyone touches you."

"Nearly murdered," I retorted.

Stella waved a hand of dismissal at me. "Then your eyes glaze like you're seeing a distant planet."

"Head injury," I countered. "Bludgeoned. Almost drowned."

Stella growled softly and grabbed my wrists. Before memory and emotions flooded me, I caught a forlorn glint in Stella's eyes. I ripped my hands away before her shame overtook me.

"That's what I'm talking about!" Stella lurched toward me in excitement. "Where did you go? What happened? Why did you pull back? Every time anyone goes to touch or hug you, you go rigid. Not normal. Even for you!"

Frustration fed my voice as I tried to stave off the internal pressure. "I almost died!" I snapped, angrier than I meant to sound. "Normal doesn't exist anymore."

Stella reached out for me and pulled her hands back before touching me. She folded them in her lap. "I know," she whimpered before clearing her throat free of sadness. "I saw it."

I blinked. "What do you mean?"

"I'm the one who found you," she explained. "I pulled you from the water. Your lips were pale blue." Stella sniffled. "It was horrible. I thought you were dead. It was too late for Miss Woods."

Tears dropped on Stella's crossed legs.

Despite my better judgment, I reached out and held Stella's hand. She placed hers on top of mine and kept talking. I heard half of what Stella said as my brain traveled to her teens and experienced her kissing Mr. Vos and the night of crying that followed. I crumbled onto my quilt when Stella retrieved her hand and left the room.

"I brought the tissues," she announced upon her return. "What's wrong?" She sat beside me gingerly this time. "Are you going to be sick? Do I need to get a trash can?" The urgency in her voice tickled me. She thought I was about to upchuck. A snort escaped as a fit of laughter overtook me. Stella followed suit.

Stress melted away until I was lightheaded from giggling. I was ready to reveal my biggest fear now. A moment after Stella's end of laughing wheeze, she started the conversation. "Tell me what brought up Mr. Vos this afternoon. I haven't thought about him for years."

I investigated her face. Stella was fibbing. "That's not true," I stated. "You feel guilty about him kissing you."

Stella cringed. "I've never told you that. I've told no one about the kiss."

"I know," I said. "I don't know why you didn't trust me enough to say something."

Stella grimaced. "We were kids."

"Yes, and he was an adult. You had a crush on him, sure. I remember you talking about him. But I had no clue he'd taken advantage of you."

Shock of me uncovering her secret had my bestie off center. She dove into her tale. "I flirted first," Stella sniffled. "It was during my vampire phase."

Stella and I were forbidden from watching vampire films or reading them as books as young teens. However, Stella snuck in a few chapters at lunch in the school library. She caught me up on the latest bloodsucking drama on Friday nights.

"So, you thought you'd start your own forbidden romance?" I asked, half teasing.

"I guess," Stella snickered through her shame. "But it was horrible. Nothing like I'd imagined. My first kiss tainted by an old man's breath and enough guilt to squash me. It felt dirty and sordid."

"It was," I rallied. "But not on your part. Especially with your mom right there."

Stella's eyes bugged. "How did you know that? How do you know all these details?"

I shrugged. "I'm getting all kinds of information I didn't ask for. It's blowing my mind." I grabbed my head.

"I cried for a month," Stella said thoughtfully as she stared into my eyes.

I ignored the questioning in her glance and pressed on. "And you stopped singing," I said, realizing how the timeline laid out. Stella stopped striving for a singing career and began studying at an esthetician school. "I always wondered why you gave it up?"

"You gave up writing," she retorted.

I laughed. "That's because I'm a horrible writer, not because my English teacher got frisky."

Stella's eyes trailed away as she detailed the incident with every new description. A weight was lifting. It wasn't good for her to carry around blame and ditch her dreams because of a weak-willed thirty-year-old man. He was lucky Stella knew how to keep a secret. I would have kicked him in the shins for hurting my friend. Through tears of sorrow and rage, a younger, peppier Stella resurfaced. My best friend grew more into herself right before me.

"It's amazing to get that all out," she sighed.

I wiped my eyes, mopping up the remnants of a crying fit. "I'm glad."

Stella sat up straighter. She looked me over. "Will it hurt you to hug me?"

My heart broke. My friend needed me, and I was stuttering about comforting her. "It would hurt me not to hug you," I answered, tossing my arms around Stella, who embraced me back.

Tears and jagged weeping continued—some for Stella and some for me. But no new scenes or feelings surfaced. I pulled away, happy.

"What's that smile for?" Stella asked. "Did you fart or something?"

I smacked her playfully. "No, you nerd."

"Then what?"

"Nothing," I explained. "Nothing happened."

Stella's eyebrow peaked. "Were you expecting something to happen?"

"Every time I touch someone today, I get these weird feelings. Like I'm downloading their deepest thoughts or secrets."

Stella's eyes bugged. "That's what's been going on?"

I pulled back. "You believe me?"

"Why wouldn't I?"

I blinked. "I've just told you I may have gained superpowers, and you're fine with it?"

Stella shrugged, non-committal. "Superpower is a strong term. We'll have to wait and see. Your intuition may be overcompensating for letting you down at the spa."

My mouth twisted sideways. "Perhaps," I said. "Maybe it'll go away."

Stella nodded. "Sleep on it," she said. "I'll camp on your couch. We'll talk more in the morning."

"Sleep sounds good," I laid back on my pillows without questioning Stella's surrender.

My exhausted brain flickered with warnings. My pal was not one to step back after receiving intriguing news. I could see she was up to something. Unfortunately, I was too wiped out to care. Whatever Stella was plotting could wait until tomorrow.

Chapter 5
Life-Altering Secrets

Crunch. I winced. Crunch. I cringed. Splash. Clank. I cracked open one eye. Stella sat cross-legged on my desk chair. She stirred a bowl of shredded wheat and almond milk before bringing it to her lips. She nodded at me as I woke more fully.

"Morning," I croaked.

Stella finished her mouthful of cereal and tossed me a protein shake. "I stole some sugar from your mom's."

"That explains your lack of marshmallows," I said, twisting the cap of my breakfast.

Stella's sugar addiction was up there with mine. However, as a teen, mine layered pounds on my average frame. Hers fueled her naturally thin body, even if it excited her imagination from time to time. I'd given up sugar two years ago, and Stella swore she never would.

"Your mom is bursting at the seams," she said. "She needs to see you."

"Is everything okay?"

Stella swallowed another spoonful of cereal. "She's fine," she said. "She's worried about you. I didn't let her come in."

"Why not?" I answered. My pulse spiked. I pictured my mother pacing the floor and tugging at her cuticles as she worried. "You know she's going to be frantic."

Stella waved her hand. "Yes," she said. "I know. We'll head over there soon. For now, I have a plan."

"A plan?" I slid out of bed and walked over to my closet. As I flicked through my wardrobe, Stella finished her breakfast bowl before continuing.

"To test your superpowers," she said, as if I was still the chubby kid running to the bus, and she was waiting for me to catch up.

"I don't think...."

"I know," Stella interrupted. "You never think you're anything special. Now, you have something extraordinary proving it. I'm not letting this opportunity slide. We're going to test your 'Secret Touch'."

"Ew," I groaned, selecting a T-shirt and yoga pants. "I don't like how that sounds."

Stella laughed. "We'll think of something better later. For now, that's all I have. You're the wordsmith. You name it."

I shuffled to the bathroom, leaving my best friend debating with the air. I didn't want to name whatever it was. I wanted it to stop. I wanted to go on with everyday life as if nothing had happened. But that would be when the police caught the guy who'd killed Miss Woods. However, Stella had other ideas, but I still wanted to be free of the whole thing.

"You'll hug your mom and see what you see," Stella's voice came closer. I could tell she was standing on the other side by the shadow, eeking under the bathroom door. "Then we'll test it."

My stomach tightened. "What if I see something I don't want to see?" I asked before turning on the sink.

Stella raised her voice to combat the running faucet. "I doubt your mom has a Mr. Vos story. Besides, you two are close. What could she possibly be hiding from you?"

I brushed my teeth. Until yesterday, I thought I knew everything about Stella. Yet, she'd sealed off a life-altering secret and moved on. If Stella could hide something from me, anyone could. I spit out my toothpaste and watched as the gob circled the drain. There was no avoiding my mother. I'd have to touch her sooner than later. Playing in Stella's laboratory might gamify an otherwise traumatic uncovering.

I rolled my shoulders and glanced at my face in the mirror. The bruise on my cheek faded to a putrid brown. A little powder would take off the gruesomeness, if not hide the damage completely. Perhaps if I looked less beaten, Mom wouldn't panic so much. It was worth a try. And as much as I hated it, Stella's scheme was worth a shot.

Chapter 6

Troubling Questions

Mom leaped from the couch and wiped her cheeks when I stepped through the sliding glass door. Her red-rimmed eyes weren't hiding anything. Mom was ending a crying jag, possibly because of my injuries.

Chills rallied up my neck. I didn't like using anyone, and to test Stella's theory, I had to make my Mom a science project. I rubbed my forearms as a million troubling questions washed over me.

What if Mom's revelations ruined our relationship? What if she could tell I was siphoning her secrets? What if it didn't work at all? What if it worked too well and my brain imploded, trying to sponge off Mom's innermost thoughts?

I swallowed back my trepidation as Mom approached with open arms. When I flinched, she frowned. She paused seconds before embracing me and gently sweeping my bangs from my face. She clicked her tongue as she peered through my cover-up at my bruise.

"My baby," Mom whimpered. "I can't imagine. I'm so glad you're safe. I've been praying about it all day."

My tears startled me. There was something about talking to my mom that made every emotion surface.

"Where's Stella," she asked, shaking us both from our sadness. "She promised not to leave your side." A twinge of frustration lingered in Mom's tone.

I was quick to correct her. "I think she transferred responsibility to you when she watched me walk over." Like I was a toddler, I thought. "She's running errands while I'm here."

"Why does that sound ominous?" Mom asked, a giggle behind her expression.

"Because it's Stella we're talking about," was my answer.

Mom's eyes softened, and she rested a hand on my knee. Her cool skin shot emotions through my limbs. I was back in a bathroom weeping over lost babies and empty cradles. When Mom looked at her reflection, she pushed past the frog in her throat to recite Hannah's Prayer from the book of First Samuel.

I rolled through every feeling as if it were my own. Guilt, sorrow, depression, self-pity, faith, worry, and victory pummeled me and made my stomach rock like a ship at sea. I blanched as an angry jealousy, not my own, washed through me.

My mom pulled back. She rushed away and returned just as quickly, carrying our family's barf bucket. I used the sick pail three times before purging the borrowed sorrow from my body, returning to myself just as Mom reached for her phone. She rattled details about head injuries and nausea as her fingers flew across the screen.

"Wait, I'm fine." I half lied.

Mom paused long enough for me to coax her back to my side. "You don't look fine," she whispered, placing her palm on my forehead like she was checking my temperature. I grabbed her wrist and set it on her lap before she could make contact.

"We need to chat," I whispered. "But I'm not sure how to start."

Mom's wide-eyed worry scanned me from head to foot and back, finally landing on my belly. It took me a moment to understand her pointed glance. "Not that," I hurried. "You know I've never dated anyone but Brett. That didn't go that far."

Mom shrugged. "I didn't want to assume."

Sure, she didn't, I thought. I jumped subjects too quickly for my mother to object. "Mom, you don't have to feel guilty over being jealous of your sister. It's natural. She had baby after baby without even trying."

Mom shot me the same inquisitive look Stella had but shook it off.

"Your father and I battled for ten years before having you," she said. "It was so hard not to feel forsaken. I hated my sister for being fertile. Isn't that horrible? But how did you know...I've only ever told your father that. What made you bring that up?"

I had to find a reason for my nosiness. Once again, I fell back on my freshest excuse, trauma. "Almost dying opened my eyes to a lot of things," I said. It was the truth.

Mom nodded. She wasn't fully convinced of my reasoning but didn't press it. Her eyes went from scrutinizing slants to stunned spheres of terror. Her bottom lip trembled as she struggled for the words to explain. Then she heaved a weighty sigh before telling me her entire story.

Chapter 7
Intriguing Points and Plans

"What happened?" Stella asked. She perched like a vulture, ready to pick at my skeleton when I returned to my tiny cottage. I slumped into the room and onto my couch. "That bad, huh?"

"Worse," I said. "I threw up."

"What? Why?" Stella unfolded and slunk onto the cushion beside me.

"It got intense," I said with a shrug. "That's the best I know how to explain it. One minute I'm hugging her and can hear her crying, even though she's not. Then I see her face reflected in a mirror as she mourns lost babies I never knew about."

"Miscarriages?" Stella asked. "That sucks."

"You're not listening. I could feel her pain as if it were my own. I heard her thoughts at the same time I was thinking and feeling my own. Talk about a dizzy fit. I yakked until I couldn't anymore."

"And now?" I knew what Stella wanted to hear.

"I can hug her, and it's almost back to normal. There's a slight static sound in my head, but nothing too bothersome."

"Is it the same with me?" Stella asked.

As I was thinking about it, Stella pounced. She wrapped me in a bear hug, ensuring her sleeveless arms met my sleeveless arms. A faint hum fell into a rhythm in the back of my mind. It was almost pleasant, like falling asleep on my Dad's shoulder as a little girl during church. The rise and fall of his breath and the rattle of his deep singing voice was once my favorite comforts. Feeling something similar in Stella's hug was a relief.

"Nothing. Just the hum."

Stella pulled back. "Thank God for that," Stella said. "Imagine if we couldn't hug anymore."

I smiled. Stella was as physically demonstrative as my mother. No wonder I loved her. "But what does it mean?" I asked, as the background noise faded.

"We'll have to test it some more, but I think it means that once you know a person's secret, you can no longer hear it. That Mr. Vos story has haunted me for years. I feel lighter now that someone knows."

"Mom told me things she said she'd only told Dad," I mumbled.

"Did she tell you before or after the voices stopped?" Stella asked.

I shivered. "Before," I said. "Let's not start calling it the voices."

"Oh, pish," Stella said. "Who should we test it on next?"

My chest tightened. "Didn't you hear me when I told you I barfed? I don't want to do it again, ever."

"You can't go your whole life without touching people." Stella put her hands on her hips.

"I can if I want to." I pouted.

"You're a masseuse!"

She was right, but that didn't mean I had to like it. What was I going to do? I couldn't work again if this new ability kept popping up. I was a massage therapist. It was my job to touch people.

"We have to test it to see how to control it. It's science," Stella said, as if science was the answer to everything.

"Science only studies the natural realm. I'm not sure my secret sponge gift is natural."

"You make an intriguing point," she said as her thumbs flew across the face of her phone. "I'm texting Steve. He'll want to see you, anyway. He called me all night to make sure you were okay."

"That's sweet," I said.

"I guess," Stella said. "For a food nerd." Her phone tweeted. "He says he can be here in two hours. He's studying or something."

"Good," I said. "I've got to rest. My head is killing me." My flippant phrase stopped me cold.

Stella locked eyes with me and set down her phone. She grabbed my hands and squeezed them.

"Never scare me like that again," she said. "I couldn't breathe when I saw you floating there, by Miss Woods."

Tears surfaced. "I'll do my best," I said as Stella's tears surfaced.

"Great." Stella swiped tears from her eyes using the back of her hand. "Now that we've settled that matter, hit the hay. We have experiments to conduct."

Chapter 8

A Cool Night with a Hot Guy

After a bottle of water, I flopped back onto my bed, wondering if it was where I'd live out the rest of my life. I'd been sleeping more than usual, and my current stress level had me yearning for my blankets.

I dreamed of walking down Deadhorse Canyon's main street on a cloudy night. The local horse and buggy taxi clopped down the cobblestone street as I strolled hand in hand with my date. I couldn't see the man's face, but I knew him to be extremely attractive and sensitive. His unspoken affection for me made my skin glow and my heart pitter-pat.

He talked to me from the depths of his being. We sprinkled everything from deep thoughts to winsome wit throughout our conversation. I longed to hold him and kiss him and hoped he'd give me a sign that he wanted the same thing. If so, I knew fireworks would fly.

I woke from my pleasant dream with a river of drool oozing down my cheek and my bestie standing above my bed. Her brother stood beside her. She smacked him in the chest. "I told you," She teased. "You're a bigger nerd than I am. You don't even have any secrets."

"What's that supposed to mean?" Steve asked. He backed away, closer to my bedroom door. I sat up and reached for a tissue to wipe away my spittle, but Stella was already at it. Testing had begun while I dreamed of a cool night with a hot man.

"I'm not allowed to sleep?" I asked, my mouth opening with a yawn.

Stella turned from her big brother to pick on me. "You've been asleep for hours. Time to get up and figure this thing out."

"Figure out what?" Steve asked, staring at us as if we'd lost our minds. Once Stella spilled the story, Steve nearly split in half from rolling his eyes too hard.

"Corky's gained superpowers," Stella said as if it were a fact.

I was just discovering my new talent. There was no telling if I'd have it long or if it would vanish as I healed. That thought had merit.

"We don't know it's a superpower," I argued. "It's probably just a glitch."

"Uh huh," Steve said. "I don't suppose either of you can expound on what this glitch does that's so super."

Stella bounced on her toes. She raised her hand like she was in third grade. "Ooh, me," she said. "I'll tell you. Can I?" She turned to me for permission, and I gave it to her. If I hadn't, she might have exploded on the spot.

"Corky can see a person's deepest secrets with a single touch." Stella giggled with excitement as if the gift was hers, not mine.

"Hilarious," Steve said. "I was in the middle of studying, and you called me over here for this?" His comment stung his sister, but then he looked at me. "You're better than this, Corks."

"Oh, stop acting so high and mighty. It's real, and it's awesome!" Stella sat on the bed next to me. She lifted my hand out to Steve. "Here, touch her. Unless you have something to hide."

"Don't be dumb," Steve said. He took a step backward, folding his arms behind his back.

"I'm not dumb," Stella said. "I'm trying to share. Plus, I need you. We need you to conduct a few experiments. You're our test tube."

"Flattering," I said, as Steve wilted into the wallpaper. "You don't have to do anything you don't want to."

"Neither do you," Steve said.

"I'm not afraid to touch you."

"Watch out, Steve," Stella said. "You've finally met a woman that wants to touch you, and you're running away."

"Perhaps I'm not interested in being part of your clinical trial," he replied.

"Stella, it's fine." I wanted to end the argument before it became heated. With Steve and Stella, one never knew. In a moment, they could switch from bantering to backhanded commenting. I guessed that's just what siblings did, but I wouldn't know.

"We'll figure out another way," I said.

Stella stuck out her tongue at her brother. "Since you're here, can you make food?" She flashed from hostile and demanding to humble and demure. Steve rolled his eyes.

"Only because I have to study, and this will help me with my practical," he said. "Or else no food for you." He pointed to Stella. "For you, Corky, I'd cook any day."

"Awe, how sweet," Stella clutched her heart. "Crushing much?"

"And that's it. There'll be no dinner for Stella. Corky, I'll run to the store and be back in a minute. "

"Don't forget, no sugar," I hollered to Steve as he left my room.

"How could I forget," Steve said. A moment later, my front door opened and closed.

"What a dork," Stella said when Steve left. "As for us, please hustle your fabulous self into the living room. I've got a few things to show you."

"Why does that terrify me?"

Chapter 9

Not Going to be Fun

My cozy living room was no longer my own. String art tracked along my main wall in diagonal patterns. A plethora of sticky notes, reusable shopping bags, and permanent markers were spread along my coffee table and cascaded to the floor. I frowned at my London fog-gray walls.

"I'm going to need to repaint," I said after counting at least twenty-five push pins stabbed into my mellow aesthetic.

"At least I used a complementing color," Stella said, referring to the happy mustard yard looped around the silver pins. It matched the gold and gray phases of the moon quilt draped on the back of my couch.

"You get a pass," I said, raising my index finger. "For now! And only because I've suffered a head injury and don't feel like arguing."

Stella ignored me. "You're going to love all of this." She spread her arm out in game show co-host fashion.

"Where do I sit?" I asked.

Stella hurried to remove a raincoat from the back of my oversized chair that I used to sit and read. I looked for the books still left on the seat. Stella transformed them into a makeshift side table, leaving iced coffee dripping down their spines.

"Stells Bells," I hollered, hurrying over to my books. Once I'd rescued them from the threat of condensation, I took my place in the seat and stared at Stella for, waiting for an explanation.

She organized a few bundles before turning her most charming grin in my direction. This is going to be bad, I thought.

"That's for you." Stella nodded to the drink sporting a half-naked straw.

"I figured," I said. "It seems like you're trying to coax me into something nefarious."

"Who? Me?"

I was doomed.

Stella straightened in her normal stance that I remembered from High

School Lit class and every other lecture she'd given me through the years. I called it the, "I'm going to give the persuasive essay" look.

"After a devastating event, you've rallied back to discover you now have a supernatural ability. What do you do?"

I didn't give an answer because Stella didn't require one. This was her rhetorical hook and next came her thesis. "One cannot live with a gift and not use it, but one must discover its boundaries and applications before they can weld it with precision and compassion."

"Weld? Really?" I rolled my eyes. "Can't you get straight to the point? I'm not Ms. Campbell. You're not getting a grade."

Stella kneeled next to my chair. "I'm so afraid you'll say no. You've got to listen with an open mind. Promise?"

I nodded. It's not like she wanted me to become Cat Woman or some other avenging hero. My gift would not defeat evil or defend the innocent. So far, its only purpose was to make me even more awkward than I already felt and to make me vomit. Good times.

"I'll do my best. But you can stop the five-paragraph report. Just cut to it. My head is still not right." I tore the remaining paper from my straw and slurped down the dark chocolate goodness. A cocoa nib melted on my tongue, giving me the punch I needed to pay attention.

"Great," Stella said with a clap. "First, we need to understand the boundaries of this touch thing."

"Boundaries?"

Stella listed them on her fingers. "Does it have limits? Can it be stopped? Is the only way to quiet it to make the subject reveal their secrets? Can we use anything to insulate you from contact?"

"Insulate? I'm not electric."

Stella snatched a post and started writing. "Great point! Perhaps you are. Maybe it's moisture in our skin that carries the charge?"

"The charge?" I said. "I think it's a temporary situation. Once my head heals, it'll be gone."

"All the more reason to figure it out the best we can before Saturday."

I paused mid-coffee slurp. "Before the memorial, you mean."

Stella batted her eyes at me. "That's why I love you. You're a quick one."

"Continue," I said as I crunched another nib.

"I thought you could go to the memorial, touch a few people, and see if any clues pop up," Stella said as if she'd handed me a grocery list and not a list of potential suspects.

"I don't think so. Touching people is the last thing I want to do." But I did want my attacker behind bars.

Stella's eyebrows knitted together as she searched for her next pitch. I watched as her pensive attitude flexed into a puppy dog-eyed pleading. "I know, but just think about it. You find the bad guy, avenge Ms. Woods, and yourself, and life can go as planned."

"Except I can touch no one ever again without encountering their guiltiest moments."

"That's where these come into play." Stella lifted the bag. "We're going to turn off your sleuthing radar. No point saving your life for you to remain a shut-in."

I frowned. "Now, we're saving my life?"

Stella got serious. "Haven't you thought about it at all?"

"Thought about what? My career being over? I've been in an undercover panic since this special gift of mine keeps spiking at will."

Stella crunched over plastic wrappers and papers. She sat on the table edge to give us a closer face-to-face. "Not just that. Your actual life. Corks, you walked in on a killer."

Fear rallied up my throat. "I didn't see anything." My voice squeaked. Somewhere in my mind, I knew I'd have to face what happened to me and Miss Woods, but I'd been running from it since I woke up in the hospital. I didn't want to remember or see or think about what happened. It was a horrifying situation I didn't want to revisit.

Stella placed her hand on my knee. The static returned a little stronger than before. "But the killer doesn't know that, does he?"

I shuddered. Stella pulled away. "This is a matter of life and death," she said.

"Miss Wood's death and my life," I said, as the truth clobbered me. Stella nodded. I'd been right. Here we go, I thought. One step deeper into trouble.

Chapter 10

A Pleather Glove

After convincing me to stalk a killer at the memorial, which freaked me out, Stella moved on to the next step in her three-part plan.

Steve arrived just in time for her to lure him into the fold. "Get your bum over here and help me," Stella said.

"I'm just here to cook the food," Steve raised his arms in the air and scooted past his little sister. He slid into my small galley kitchen and set down his bags.

Steve stared at the bare concrete countertops and empty yellow cabinets. I was trying to give up my binging ways. Making my kitchen appealing to the eyes was one way to sabotage that struggle. "Don't worry," he said as if I was at all concerned with his kitchen woes. "I brought all my gear."

He stepped outside to wheel in a wagon of appliances, knives, and other cooking ware. "No chef Mike tonight," he said, mostly to himself, referring to the microwave.

"No Chef Steve either, unless you help me first."

Steve frowned at Stella. "Let me get the oven preheating, and then I can help,"

"Then I'll explain as you work," she said. "In these bags, I have many accessories that I hope will help Corky turn off her gift."

Steve guffawed. "Are you still pulling that one? I thought leaving would shake you both out of it."

Stella glared at her brother. "Listen, Mr. Tall Hat, I'll prove it to you. I had wanted you to be the one to do this, but I've thought of a way around it."

"You came up with another deep dark secret?" I asked.

Stella chuckled. "Since last night," she said. "I wish. Though not the same kind I shared last night."

"I missed something," Steve said.

"That's normal." Stella waved off her brother. "Give me five minutes, and then pay attention as you prep."

"Whatever you say," Steve said.

Stella left Steve and me alone in my living room. "Do you have any clues?" I asked him.

"If I did, I couldn't tell you," he said. "You're the secret seer, remember?"

I clicked my tongue and winked at Steve. "We'll see."

Stella returned to the room with a smug smile stamped on her face. "I've got a secret," she said, standing on her toes, which meant she was amped up and excited. The stance didn't happen often. New boys, delectable desserts, and Christmas presents were the most common inciters of the pose. The secret she had must be a juicy tidbit.

"Great," I said. "So, do I touch you now?" I rose.

"Slow your roll," she said. "Dig in that bag and snag a pair of gloves. I'm going to tell Steve what my secret is."

"Won't that defeat the purpose?" Steve asked.

"Not if I write it on a sticky note, food boy." Stella mocked. She scribbled on a notepad and handed it to her brother.

"You didn't," he said. Shock flushed his face.

"Shush," Stella said. "No spoilers!"

She walked over to me. Her long legs and bare arms made me nervous. "Just a short touch," I said. "I don't want to barf."

"Okay," Stella said. Her face fell as if I'd just farted on her pillow. "But soon, we'll have to test that limit too."

"How about never testing it," I said.

Steve gagged. He had a very delicate sympathetic reflex. I remembered it triggering him quite a few times as kids. "Please don't," he said. "I don't want to ruin dinner."

"Fine," Stella said. "But you're both babies. This is for science."

Steve and I locked glances. Steamroll Stella was on the move. She wouldn't stop until she'd had her say and usually her way, too. We loved the pushy lady, but running out of her way was tiring.

"You control the time," Stella said. She stuck out her arm in front of me.

I reached out a single finger and tapped the top of her arm. A swirling sensation took me over, but no whispers came. That's when her voice took over my head. Stella giggled. A flood of mischief clouded over me. Then my mind's vision cleared, and I could see her.

"You wiped a booger on my hoodie!" I ripped my hand away from her. "Are you out of your mind?"

"You're just now asking that after fifteen years of friendship?" Steve asked as he chopped something that sounded like lettuce in the kitchen.

Stella bent over with laughter. She wheezed but found the strength to straighten back up. "How long did that take?" she asked.

"I didn't have a timer going, but it felt like thirty seconds. Maybe more, but less than a minute."

"Well, there's that then. Let's practice with gloves," Stella said.

"I already know what you're trying to hide from me," I said. "How will we find out what works if you don't have any secrets?"

I heard Steve drop something into a bowl, but couldn't see it, though it smelled lovely. Stella turned to him. "I'm still not doing this," he said. "And it'll take more than a booger to convince me she sees secrets."

"Then hang on tight," Stella said. "I was in her room for ten minutes. There's a lot of trouble I could get into in that amount of time."

I dropped my head in my hands. Thank goodness Stella brought me a coffee. I hadn't known at the time it was for sustenance and not a bribe. "Let's get this over with."

The secrets kept coming no matter what we tried.

Latex didn't work-Stella had hidden all my underwear under my bed.

Dish gloves didn't work- She moved all my bookmarks from their places.

Mittens were a no-go-She'd stolen my favorite dragonfly earrings.

Work gloves failed- Stella kissed my picture of Indiana Jones while wearing my favorite hot pink lip gloss. Finally, after many tries, I slid on a pair of vegan leather black gloves.

"I look like an ill-equipped bank robber," I said, holding my hands for Stella to inspect them.

"Especially in this heat," Steve said. He'd stopped preparing minutes ago and leaned against the fridge, watching the show.

"Nobody cares how you look," Stella said. "Now, grab me."

I started with a single finger but then wrapped my entire hand around Stella's forearm. There was no buzzing. No feelings invaded. No images flickered.

"They work!" I leaped to my feet and hugged Stella, forgetting my power.

Her thoughts and actions pummeled me. "You read my diary!" I slapped her with a throw pillow.

She cackled. "Five entire pages."

Steve's face fell. "This is real," he said. "Corky can read people's minds."

"Told you!" Stella did a victory dance in her brother's face while I slid off the pleather glove and stared at my hands.

Chapter 11
Ready, Set...

"Remind me why we're here again?" I asked Stella as Steve drove us to Deadhorse Canyon Cemetery for the memorial. I'd thought it would occur at a church or community center, when I agreed to go. Graveyards gave me the chills.

"We're paying respects to Miss Woods and looking for her killer. All the true crime podcasts say it's common for the murderer to insert themselves into the aftermath of their crimes." Stella spoke as if it were her life on the line.

"Yes," Steve said. "However, the same person who killed Miss Woods is the same person who tried to kill Corky. I'm going to repeat my plea. Let's not do this."

"Do you have a better idea?"

"Maybe have the police handle it?" Steve said.

Stella waved off the suggestion. She pulled down the visor and checked her makeup in the mirror. "Corks has on a floppy hat and large shades. No one will recognize her. Especially the person who tried to kill her. She won't look like herself at all."

Stella had a stellar way of making me even more worried than I was before. Steve caught my anxiety. He leaned closer and said, "Stay by me. I'll protect you."

Stella snorted and then calmed herself. "It's a good idea, Corks. Stay by the Wookie cookie here, and I'll stalk the attendees."

I didn't feel great about letting Stella wander the gravesite alone but staying in the shadows was ideal. Steve would be there. He could always get me out of trouble before it boiled over. At least, I hoped so.

Stella strutted along the green in strappy high heels. Her skirt sashed as she navigated the grassy area. I stood back, waiting.

"We'll wait until the preacher prays," Steve said. Was it me, or did he scoot farther onto his side of the truck?

"Sounds good. I don't want anyone to touch me."

"Stella's heart is in the right place, but this is a small town. People are going to know who you are and what happened to you. The hugs and poor things will be inescapable. Especially for the sole survivor of the attack."

"That's what I'm afraid of," I said. "Too much, and I'll toss my oatmeal all over the casket."

"If you do, I'll carry you out of here," Steve said, adding a tiny flex to his offer. He smiled. "It's a joke."

I reached a hand to my face. "Do I look that freaked out?"

"Kind of," Steve said, trying to comfort me. "Do you have your gloves?"

I looked at my lap. "They would look better if this were winter. In summer, I look like a serial killer." My words flared up, and the new fear rested in the pit of my stomach. It burned like an ulcer. Finding Miss Woods's killer would help it go away, right? I hoped so and maybe my gift would fade away with it.

"She's flagging us," Steve said.

He popped open his truck door and hurried to open mine. Steve was always doing stuff like that. It made him endearing to my mother, respectable to my father, and annoying to his sister. I liked it. Even in High School he never failed to hold a door for me. I felt like an undercover princess in his company.

"Thanks," I said. I secured my skirt as I slid down from the truck. Steve took my hand in his. "You're wearing gloves, too?"

"Didn't want you to stand out too much," he said.

I was touched. "Thank you."

Steve shut the door and waited for me to start up to the crowd above us. I didn't want to be there. Just as confidence replaced trepidation and a familiar hate-filled voice interrupted my peace.

"Well, if it isn't, little miss victim," Melinda said. She leaned against a tree, glowering at me. Brett Booker stood close beside her. I tried to walk past without causing a scene. Melinda would have none of that. "Here to get the attention you've always craved?"

Stella burst from the crowd and got in Melinda's face. "Jealous?" Stella asked Mel. "If you'd done your job that night, you might have had the honor. But like always, you left your dirty work for Corky and me."

"Stay out of it, Yella Stella." Mel used the nickname the school used to chant at my best friend. Once upon a time, Stella was shy and awkward. Come ninth grade, her curves and courage grew in, but the nickname never faded out.

"You're such a cliche, Melinda."

I trudged over to the battle, though it was the last thing I wanted to do on a long list of things I wished I could avoid. Steve was right behind me, his hands behind his back. It was Brett who ended the fight.

"Mel, this isn't the place," he said. Brett Booker, my ex-boyfriend, looked me up and down. Worry creased his forehead. Was that worry for me or Mel, the girl who stole him from me?

"Are you taking their side?" Mel snapped. She turned to him with heat coming off her painstakingly made-up face.

"I'm thinking of Miss Woods," Brett answered.

Mel glared at Brett and then turned her spite toward the rest of us. In a flicker, her malice faded, and her fake smile returned. "For Miss Woods then," she said, "Though I still say Corky faked the whole thing. She probably tripped on those ape-ish feet of hers."

"Melinda..." Brett said. He wrapped an arm around her waist. I could still remember what that felt like when he held me. His affection made me feel like I could fly. Now, I wondered if he touched me, what dark secrets would spill from Brett's self-consciousness.

"I know," Mel said sweetly. "For Miss Woods."

Stella returned to my side and linked her arm in mine. The skin-to-skin made the buzzing return. It was soothing after Melinda's attack. When I turned to face the mourners, all eyes were on me. Thankfully, the preacher started the memorial, and my gawkers tuned into his words.

Chapter 12
GO!

The memorial was good as far as memorials go. A large number of people cried, and nice words were said. I wept for Miss Woods and would've cried more if not for everyone was staring at me. They hid their glances, but not well. Shooting me with looks from their peripherals wasn't a good sign from the townsfolk of Deadhorse Canyon. My bravery shriveled.

At the final amen, the hounds let loose and headed straight for me. Steve reached out with a gloved hand and pushed me behind him. "I think we should head for the truck," he said.

"Yes, I think that's a good idea."

Stella ran interference as Steve raced beside me. We ran fast enough to get to the truck but not so quickly as to be rude. After all, the town didn't know I'd become a freak overnight. They just wanted news as they pretended to sympathize.

My pleather glove hit the truck's handle as another hand grabbed my shoulder. My bare shoulder.

"Nothing like a funeral to make me want a cigarette," The voice said. "Especially Emma's. Who'd want to kill Emma?"

Grief mingled with terror within me. I froze. I couldn't shake the hand away. Thankfully Stella did that for me.

"Can we help?" She asked.

I turned to see the nurse from the hospital. "That's what I wanted to ask you. Do you remember me?"

"Yes, you're my nurse. I'm sorry I don't remember your name.

"I'm Cory Tunic." Nurse Tunic held out her hand. I shook it, happy to have my gloves on. "It's nice to see that you're out and about. Even if this is the place you went." Nurse Tunic nodded toward the gravesite.

"I liked Miss Woods," I said. "I would've been here no matter what."

"Isn't that sweet," the nurse said.

Behind her, Valerie Hewitt approached and wrapped me in a bear hug.

"I told them to get him to help. I even called the county, but they won't do it," she said to someone unseen and unheard. "I don't know what else to do. The police? Only as a last resort."

A dream-like sensation flooded me with deep worry and concern. The longer Mrs. Hewitt held me, the less I could hear her real voice and the more the image zoomed out. I saw her scrolling on a legal pad beside an open file folder. The name Brandon was scrawled in red marker. And just like that, she let go, and I spiraled. I curled over with my head between my knees, searching for air.

"Is she okay?" Mrs. Hewitt worried.

"I think it's anxiety from the incident." Stella quickly covered for me.

Mrs. Hewitt clicked her tongue as she thought. "She should book an appointment to come and see me," she said. "No charge, of course. We want her to heal up and get back to life. After what she saw and went through, it may take some time. Talking to someone will help. Even if it's not me."

This time Steve stepped in. "I'll remember to discuss it with her," he said.

Nurse Tunic chimed in with her opinion. "She looks green. I better take her pulse."

"No," I said too slowly.

Cory Tunic had my glove off and her fingers on my wrist seconds before I spoke. More voices and strolls down the past washed over my mind.

"No," The nurse said. An angry man stood in front of her. I couldn't make out his face. "There is no one by that name here." She was lying. Her remorse was palatable, as was her dread. "You can talk to my boss, but she'll tell you the same thing. No one by that name is here at the moment." Her conscience didn't squeeze her as tightly over this fib. The nurse was doing something wrong for the right reasons, she told herself.

Her hand fell from mine, and a deep inhale made me woozy. Steve steadied me. I was thankful, once again, he'd thought about wearing gloves. Though he wasn't a deep-secret guy, I wasn't sure I could take any more memory flashes.

Stella opened the truck door and shoved me into the seat. "I think she needs to go home. This has been a lot."

Nurse Tunic and Mrs. Hewitt agreed. They watched me with troubled expressions as Steve pulled out of the parking lot.

Chapter 13

Grandma's Table

I soaked in a lavender chamomile bath with a cup of peppermint matcha at my side. After the double whammy at the cemetery, my stomach was churning. It spun and spiraled whenever I thought about what had happened. I fought to recall anything from my encounter with the nurse and the therapist but couldn't without dry heaving.

Giving in to the crazy that was my new life, I let myself drift in the frothy water.

Meanwhile, Stella and her brother were up to something in my living room. I could hear shuffling and knocking on the wall shared by my bathroom and living room. I turned up my spa sounds playlist and let the sound of water, crickets, and fog horns take me away from the day I was living.

It surprised me how easily I could sink into the bath. I thought after nearly drowning, I'd hate water. Instead, it called to me. Was I masochistic, or had the murder attempt left me too tired to care? Maybe the worst breakdown was yet to come.

Someone had tried to kill me. Should I have feelings about that? I witnessed someone die as I was being held under. Still, I was numb to it. Shock was the word I replayed in my mind. Truly, I didn't believe it. Something about my strange, new gift was protecting me from my current trauma. It would catch up. I just hoped I was home when it did.

Minutes later, the noise from the living room ceased. It was safe for me to come out of hiding. I secured my robe and wrapped a yellow towel in my hair. My cloudy sunshine decor calmed me. I loved the coziness of my cottage and couldn't imagine living elsewhere.

Home was my happy place until I entered my living room. Stella stood in the kitchen with Steve finishing the Caprese salad from the night before. She offered me half her plate when she saw me. Steve watched me walk in and averted his eyes. He cleared his throat and turned from me. My robe made him nervous. How cute.

"I'm dressed under my robe," I told him. "Tank top and shorts. One hundred percent modest. Promise." I lifted four fingers in a makeshift scout salute.

Steve settled. "Good to know. Wouldn't want a wardrobe malfunction. All that skin," he started but didn't finish the thought.

"Cool it, turbo," Stella said. "Can you eat?"

I shook my head. "Don't think my stomach will tolerate it, but thank you. You guys chow down. I'm good. I'm just going to lounge on the couch."

I turned around to see Stella's yarn masterpiece had grown. "What in the..." Curses and fretful phrases came to my mind. I walked closer to the loud piece. "These are pictures of the crime scene."

It overwhelmed me. I hadn't taken a bite since the memorial. My gut dropped.

"I know. Aren't they brilliant?" Stella said after swallowing her salad.

"It's terrifying!"

I caught Steve ribbing his sister with his elbow from my side-eye. She smacked him back. "I told you. It's too much too soon."

"It's too much ever," I said after catching sight of Ms. Woods covered with a spa towel. Though I couldn't see her, I knew what lay beneath the terry cloth. Bulging eyes filled with fear. Blue lips spread, desperately struggling for air that wouldn't come, and blood caked in her hair.

I bent in half. Steve ran to me. He snatched me by the elbows and lowered me to the couch cushions. His voice muffled as my power reached through my bathrobe to sift out his secrets. Steve noticed my mood change and swiftly released me.

Leave it to Steve to take care of me without overstepping. I'd tell him he was a sweetheart, but that would make him beyond uncomfortable.

I curled into myself as memories of that night overwhelmed me. The smell of shower cleanser mixed with essential oils stung my nose. My eyes watered. From tears or smells, I couldn't tell. I put my hand to my head. My bruise was still tender.

"Don't you remember anything about the killer?" Stella asked. Her voice quieted and softened as she sat beside me on the couch.

"The only secrets I can't access are my own."

Stella hugged me close. The buzzing hum returned but no secrets. Stella had emptied herself of purposeful hidings, and now she could comfort me without extra effects.

Steve backed away. He tried to console his tears, but I heard him sniffling. My held-back grief surfaced one toe at a time as if it were testing to see if I could handle it. I snuggled into Stella's shoulder and let loose. She stroked my hair and held me until I was finished sobbing. Almost dying had left its mark on me in more ways than I could imagine.

"Are you ready?" Stella asked.

"Stells Bells," Steve whispered. "Be careful."

"Of course," she said, putting away her snarky voice. Her caring best-friend tone was out to play. "Let's start with my list."

"Your list?" I asked, rubbing my eyes free of tears.

"Good thing I ran out and got you this," Steve opened my fridge, which I could see from my couch. Prepackaged homemade snacks lined the shelves. Beside them sat big leafy green salads and one dark chocolate miracle.

"Is that a cold brew?" I asked and reached my hand out to receive it. Steve slipped on his gloves and retrieved my liquid brain fuel. "Thanks for the gloves," I said when he handed them to me.

"Anything for you, Corks," he whispered, almost too low for me to hear.

"Let's sit at your table," Stella said. "That way, my crime web won't distract you."

"Crime web?" I asked. "Is that what you call this?" I motioned to the yarn and photo mess overtaking my wall. I was careful not to look at it.

"What would you call it?" Stella asked.

She rose to lead me to my sunshine yellow Formica table. It had been a housewarming present from my grandmother, who'd refurbished her kitchen table and passed it along to me. Grandma was why I loved coffee so much. Even knowing she was gone, sitting at her table made me feel safe. Sitting there now, even when confronting a murderer, had the same effect.

Chapter 14
Could It Be

S tella ran her finger down her
five-by-eight legal pad, examining
her list. There were a few names
highlighted in pink. "I think it's best to
ignore people we know couldn't have
committed the crime."

"Like who?" I asked. "I didn't see
anything. It could have been a man or
a furious woman. That leaves everybody
on that list."

"Yes, but some people have obvious
alibis. Like, Nurse Tunic was at work.

Also, Betsy, Claire, and Candice were working at Fritters and Jitters. I saw them myself when I picked up your coffee. I'm talking about people like that. Not everyone had an opportunity. Even if they left work to get to Miss Woods, they wouldn't have made it there and away without being seen."

"Fair enough," I said. "Continue."

"The obvious names are Mr. Hewitt, Melinda, and me. We were the ones who had access and opportunity. "

I snickered. "The Hewitts, no way. You come on. But Mel, I can see taking out someone who looked at Brett in a flirty way. She's hyper-protective of her hold on him."

"Yes, but Miss Wood was Brett's advisor, not just the High School's history teacher. People forget she was a student counselor too. It was her primary job. She only moonlighted as the history and government teacher."

The wheels turned in my mind. "I forgot that. She wasn't my counselor or yours."

Steve chimed in eagerly. " She served students with last names A through G. Booker."

"I wonder if she had anything to do with Brett's and my breakup and him clinging onto Mel?" I whispered. The past was the past, but it still stung. I'd never wanted Brett back. Who could love someone who left them because of their looks? Even though I'd dropped the fluff a year later, it didn't excuse him from using "Porky Corky" until he found someone more slender to date. "I hated that nickname," I whispered, though I hadn't relayed my memories aloud. She knew me well enough to understand where my mind trailed.

Stella touched me. "Back to the case and away from Booker. Mel may have been jealous of Ms. Woods. I could see that."

I pictured Mel thwacking Miss Woods and holding her underwater until she stopped flailing then getting a secret glee from repeating the process on me. Could it be Mel?

"She had an opportunity? All she'd have to do is hang out in a therapy room and wait," Stella said.

Steve sat beside Stella after sliding a bowl of cottage cheese, peaches, and honey before me. "Eat," he said.

"Thanks," I answered, unsure if my stomach could handle more. I took a small bite, then said, "Was her car there when you arrived?"

Stella's eyes rolled toward the ceiling as she drew on her memory. "So much happened," she said. "I don't remember the outside of the spa, but the inside. And you." Her voice frogged. "I kind of forgot everything else."

"Except to take pictures," Steve said, pointing to the crime web.

"That was after she was okay," Stella said, as if Steve was making a fuss over nothing.

"Define okay." What Stella may see as okay might have been the end of me.

Stella pursed her lips. "You doubt me? Someone tried to kill you. Once you breathed and the first responder arrived, I took pictures and sank into the background. You were perfectly safe, and you know they wouldn't let me in after they cleared you off the scene."

Steve rolled his eyes and leaned back in his chair. "Did you even try to pull Miss Woods from the pool?"

Stella's eyes shot ice daggers. "I'm no monster!" She shifted the subject. "Back to Mel. She had the opportunity. Her prints would naturally be at the scene."

"So are yours," Steve hissed.

"No one's going to suspect me," Stella said, waving a hand at me. "Corky's my best friend. No one would ever find me guilty of killing her. But Mel's a distinct flavor of cookie. She's like a raisin in your chocolate chip, a betrayer through and through. Murdering Corky is probably her favorite daydream. There's one motive. Then Miss Woods and Brett were super tight. After all these years, she's his career advisor."

Steve spat. "What career? Brett's been everything in Deadhorse Canyon or tried to be. After ditching Corks and hooking up with Mel, he can't decide. What career is he aiming for now?"

My answer came automatically. "Grief counselor," I said. "Don't ask how I know."

Stella leaned over to whisper, not quietly, to Steve. "Miss Woods isn't the only person from Brett's past he asks for advice."

"No," Steve said. He turned to face me. "And you let him?"

I shrugged. "It's a bad habit," I said. "He emails me to ask for advice, that's all. I don't talk to him or meet him face to face."

"But you give him advice?" Steve said. "Come on, Corks. You're better than that."

"I know," I said, understanding his point. It was one Stella made for me often. "Maybe I'll change my email address and start over."

"Hallelujah!" Stella clapped. "We have a breakthrough. When this is over, I will hold you to it."

I sipped my coffee. "Who else is on the list?" When the cool caffeine slid onto my tastebuds, my mind returned to my flash with Mrs. Hewitt and Nurse Tunic. "Anyone named Brandon on that list?"

Stella scrolled through the names. "Not that I recognize," she said.

"Starting with Mel, then?" Steve asked.

"What choice do we have?" And my nightmare continued.

Chapter 15

Chatting with the Raisin

It took a heap of pep talks to get my feet padding up the walkway to Melinda's house. Her parents left it to her after graduation, when they moved to Europe. I wasn't one to poke at spoiled children. I lived rent-free in the cottage behind my parent's house. However, Melinda enjoyed making people believe she was super successful all on her own. Although, I'd never met a receptionist, five years after high school, as monetarily ahead as she claimed to be.

I knocked on her front door with clenched fists before calming myself down by muttering to myself. "I'm here to help me and Miss Woods. I'm here to help me."

Encouraging words melted to fear when Mel opened the door. She was as cute as ever, even in yoga shorts and a sports bra. It made me feel small, seeing her in workout clothes. She glittered in sweat. When I worked out, I turned red and blotchy. Instead, she glistened and glowed.

"What do you want?" she asked.

My nerves lost me. "I wanted to talk about the day of the attack."

Melinda rolled her eyes. "Of course you do," she said. To my surprise, she opened the door widely and asked me inside. My gut kicked at me. If she truly was the murderer, the last place I should be was alone with her in her house.

"No," I told myself. "I was here because there was no way Melinda was a killer." That thought trailed away when I noticed how muscular Melinda really was. Her workouts worked wonders on her slim figure. She was far from frail and frilly. But was she ripped enough to hold Miss Woods underwater?

"Thanks," I said as Melinda closed the door and sealed me into her web. She led me to her back porch. Outdoor misters cut through the summer morning sun.

"Want tea?" she asked. "I only have unsweetened oolong. None of that junk you put into your body."

I ignored the half-dig. "I'd love a glass."

Melinda's head twitched in surprise. "I'll be right back. Have a seat."

I watched in shock as Mel walked away, trusting me alone on her porch. I helped myself to her patio furniture and relished the cooling mist as it landed on me.

Melinda returned moments later and handed me a tall glass of tea with a spring of mint as a garnish. My mouth dropped open.

"Don't act so surprised," Melinda said as she sat in the lounge across from mine. "I have manners."

Manners she used on everyone else but me, I thought.

"Besides, oolong burns calories. Hence the large glass for you."

And there was Melinda I loved to loathe. "Very thoughtful," I said.

Melinda nodded before taking the time to appraise me. Not aiming or nonchalance, she scanned me from head to foot. "Mind telling me why you're dressed like something from a Tim Burton film? It's ninety degrees and sticky."

I knew how hot it was in my long-sleeved black shirt, leggings, combat boots, and gloves. My look did not fit the climate.

"Mourning?"

Melinda's smirk returned. "Leave it to you to sop up every bit of sympathy you can get as if it were gravy, and you were a dry biscuit."

"Gross," I couldn't help but comment. Melinda loved tossing food references into her digs about my past. It never made sense. How could she despise me both for being fat once and also for slimming down? Brett Booker was the likely answer.

"Move along," Melinda said. "Tell me why you're sitting on my porch, drinking my tea? What do you want to know about last Friday?"

What did I want to know? "Anything, I guess."

"Anything? Like?"

"Maybe if you saw anything strange. Did anyone make last-minute appointments?"

"You've always been strange. The Hewitts switched their appointments. You and your partner in crime messed up my pristine planner and screwed up my day. So, I cut out at the end of my shift and went to an appointment of my own. You had to clean up alone."

Hearing her state her snubs so blatantly chilled me. It was all a reminder of how much Melinda despised me. "Stella and I had nothing to do with your planner other than erasing the "S" from Mrs. Hewitt's Mrs."

"Don't be dumb," Melinda said before sipping her water. "A page has been missing for almost a week. Crossing out Mrs. Hewitt's was the last straw in a long list of grievances."

"You have grievances?"

Melinda sipped her water again. "More than I feel like listing to you, today."

"So why are you talking to me if you have so many 'grievances'?" I asked and downed half of the oolong tea.

Melinda paused her insulting manner for a long moment. She finished her water as she gathered her thoughts. "Because" she said. "It could've been me. If I hadn't ditched you, it would've been me."

Chapter 16
Your Fault

I strolled back to my house in a haze. As I passed the friendly houses of unknown neighbors, I was stunned. First, Melinda was semi-nice to me. That was enough to shock anyone with a cursory knowledge of our relationship.

Then there was the simple realization that if I hadn't been cleaning the steam room and showers, Mel would have taken the hit, most literally, for me. I reached to the back of my head, feeling the still-incensed bump. Ponytails and loose braids would be my trademark until it healed. Would my "gift" fade as my bruise did?

The next brainwave to strike was how dumb it had been to walk to Melinda's. Walking was my primary mode of transport. Deadhorse Canyon was small enough to negotiate with nothing more mechanical than a two-wheeler.

In my equestrian hometown, most of the neighbors took their horses everywhere. Since losing weight, I used walking to and from places as exercise. But walking, in all black, on a humid day was pure stupidity. I peeled off my gloves and shoved them into my pocket.

I couldn't wait to get home and rinse the horse trail dust and sweat off me. Three blocks to go, I told myself, but it wasn't encouraging. I'd been shuffling for the last ten minutes. Gravity increased with each step as the horrid summer weather beat down on me.

It took triple my normal time to make it home in the sludgy sun. Though I hadn't invited her, seeing Stella seated in my only outdoor furniture, a rocker, wasn't surprising.

"Too hot to talk," I wheezed, sliding my key into the front door lock.

"No wonder," Stella said, appraising my get-up. "Is it vampire day in Deadhorse Canyon?"

Once inside and the climate-controlled air hit my face, I could suck in a full breath. I helped myself to a bottle of water before talking. "Melinda said I looked Goth, too," I said. "But not a vampire. Leave that to you."

"One can always hope," Stella said, cocking her head to the side in a playful teenie bopper stance. She batted her lashes at me. Here it came. More news or another request. "So..." she said, hoisting herself onto the kitchen countertop.

"Melinda's Melinda," I said as I refilled my water. "She's bitter, mean, and a little scared."

"She said that?"

"Melinda would never say that. Not to me. No, but she looked that way, and I don't know why?"

"Maybe she's afraid she'll be caught." Stella's voice went up an octave at the thought of Melinda in jail. I pictured Stella, thinking of Mel in an orange jumpsuit. My bestie hadn't the smallest of soft spots for the woman who'd stolen my man.

I didn't like Melinda either. Sure, her stealing my boyfriend stung. However, wasn't cheating on me Brett's fault and not so much Melinda's? This was something I rarely brought to Stell's attention. She'd only guffaw it.

"I still don't see Melinda doing this thing. Especially after talking to her."

"But did you touch her skin?"

I shivered and shook my head. "You make it sound so slimy."

Stella shrugged. "You know it isn't. Why didn't you try it? Couldn't catch her?"

"I wasn't chasing her down. She offered me tea on her back porch."

"Melinda Carlie invited you in for a snack?"

I frowned at my friend. "Never a snack. A drink. Melinda Carlie doesn't snack."

"She probably doesn't poop either."

With that proclamation, Stella plopped onto my couch. She scrolled through her social media as if there weren't crime scenes pinned to the wall beside her.

I finished my second bottle of water and walked to my room. "Why didn't you go with me to Melinda's if you think she's so guilty?" I asked as I peeled off my black garb. Leaving my door open would give me more than enough space to be modest but still hear Stell's response.

"Debbie Griffle needed a facial."

"You went to Hands-On?" Panic swarmed my stomach. I couldn't imagine going back to the spa. Though I know, I'd need to one day. If so, it'd be at gunpoint by Stella in the name of sleuthing.

"Don't be silly," Stella said. "I went to her house. This girl's gotta work. I couldn't use my steamer, but Debbie had a small one. Plus, I got her to buy an entire skincare set last month. She had everything I needed."

I wrapped a towel around me and headed to the shower. Cold water awaited. Little did I know, Stella's scowl awaited me as well. "Still think Melinda Carlie is innocent?"

Stella held up her cell phone. Playing out on the Deadhorse Canyon News Now page, was an irate Melinda, still in her workout clothes. The cursing spewing from her demure mouth made me cringe. As did the one line she made sure the videographer caught straight on.

"I know you're watching this, Corky Hobbs!" Her shouting washed her neck with red, fiery anger. "Just know, I blame you for this. It's all your fault." She jammed a flawlessly manicured nail at the camera and let loose with enough F-bombs to sink a battleship.

Meanwhile, Stella cackled in my hallway, smiling at her phone screen at Melinda's arrest.

"It's not funny." I stomped my foot.

"It sort of is," Stella said. "If Melinda isn't a killer, it would be hard to prove it now. She just blamed the sole survivor as she's getting arrested."

I pulled my towel tighter and stepped past Stella. "Still not funny. I've got to do something about this."

Stella pulled her eyes away from her phone and flung her arms. "I've been saying that from the beginning! Superpowers, here we come."

"Only if I have to," I said. I shoved my friend out of the way and shut the bathroom door.

My reflection grimaced as my brown hair dropped from the bun I'd wrapped it in to visit Mel. Sweat had iced over my skin, leaving an oily sheen. But that wasn't what had me frowning.

Could I clear Melinda and solve a murder? Would Melinda accept my help? Even scarier, would the killer see me coming and finish the job? I didn't dare take a second glance at my face. I knew what awaited there—nothing but bone-shattering, heart-stopping, knee-knocking fear. I had to kick its tail and rescue my nemesis.

"Yay, me," I whimpered, as I turnedon the shower.

Chapter 17
Friendly Neighborhood Sheriff

Small towns have their perks. One is that everyone knows everyone else. Trent Gardner was no exception. He grew up down the street from my family. He was a grade below me in high school, and since then, he'd done more with his life than I had, at least from the outside. Trent got married and bought his own home. He also worked as a shared deputy between the three small towns in the area. Lucky for me, this week was his week for Deadhorse Canyon.

"Doesn't Trent have a wife to bring him lunch?" Stella asked, eyeing my bribery attempt.

"Yes," I answered. Stella wanted to see me use my newfound "magic." "He also has a three-month-old set of twins."

"Meaning?" She parked the truck as we talked.

"I'm guessing many of the newlywed vibes have dwindled, and Victoria, his wife, probably doesn't have time or energy to pack him a lunch."

"He's a grown boy," Stella said. "Can't he pack his lunch?"

"Able to and willing to are two separate things. Besides, didn't you hear the whole twin thing? He's got to be exhausted."

Stella groaned but held the door to the sheriff's office open for me. I carted in two Belly Up Burgers Double Bacon Cheeseburgers, and sides of onion rings. They were a favorite on the menu, and something that even I had to cave to now and then. I was betting Trent would be no different.

Trent met us in the foyer, a growl perched on his lips. "What do you want?" he asked.

"I brought," I began, but Trent didn't let me finish.

"A bribe?" Trent started. "So you can see Melinda? What do you think this is, a small-town mystery show? No one sees Melinda."

My mouth dropped open. This stuff always worked in books. Trent didn't even let me get a word out before slamming my hope against the wall as if it were a bent locker door.

"I just thought," I said.

Stella covered her mouth, stifling a snicker. I didn't see what she found so hilarious. This was my life, and if I didn't solve this crime, I'd be killer bait forever and have this funky gift besides.

"Trent," Stella said after calming herself. "Sure, we want to see Melinda. But ask yourself why. We hate Melinda." Stella gestured between herself and me. "Sure, we brought you lunch, but that doesn't mean..."

Trent pointed to the bag. "You brought me grease," he said. "I don't eat that stuff. Haven't since high school, and you shouldn't either." He reached for the brown sack.

I pulled the bag close as if I were protecting a baby. "Well, if you don't want it, maybe Melinda will."

That gave him pause. Melinda would eat dirt if it didn't have carbs or sweeteners. I strongly doubted a huge burger would do it for her. Hopefully, Trent didn't know that. He scratched his head and checked his watch.

"It is twelve, fifteen," he began. "I have to get her something to eat by one pm," Trent told himself. Every word spurred on the effort.

"Why go out in the heat?" Stella suggested. "You've got food here."

"And if she doesn't like it?" Trent asked. "Or complains?"

Stella's eyes sparkled. "Serves her right," she said. "Remember all those wimp jokes she tossed at you in high school? Maybe there's nothing a lawman like you can do to exact revenge. That doesn't mean we can't poke the bear a smidgen."

Trent thought a moment longer. "I'll bring her out to my desk," he said. "That way, I don't have to stand in the cell with you all."

"Thanks," Stella said.

Trent whispered to himself as he plodded down the hallway to cells unseen from the visitor's area.

I looked at Stella. "Sweetness only works in the movies," she said. "Pettiness works in real life."

With that sad thought lingering, Trent marched a raging Mel around the corner and to his desk. One passing glance was all it took for Mel to shoot daggers at me and Stella. She was beyond livid.

"Why'd you let those two freak shows in the door?" Her words sizzled with venom.

Trent's smile grew wide and wicked. "They brought you lunch." His voice sing-songed in contrast to his facial expression. Melinda didn't seem to pick up on it. She continued her snarling.

"When's my lawyer coming?" she asked Trent.

"As soon as your daddy can call him," he said as he cuffed Melinda's hand to the arm of a chair. "Speaking of," he said. "I have a call to make as well." Trent turned to the office's receptionist slash dispatcher. "Gertie," he said. "Monitor these three."

Trent nodded as he allowed Stella and me entry behind the front desk. "Five minutes then, scat."

Stella saluted him and led me back to Melinda, who was desperately attempting to get her non-bothered mask back in place. She failed.

"What did you two idiots bring me?" Melinda gestured toward the bag.

"There's one cheeseburger for you and one for Gertie," Stella said.

"And onion rings," I added.

"Saturated fat and garbage." Melinda turned up her nose at our humble offering.

Stella pulled the bag closer to her. "More for me."

"No, wait," Melinda said. "Stress makes me hungry."

I couldn't help but make a face. The woman had done nothing but judge me from the moment we met. That was before she dated Brett. Now things were much worse between us. Whenever a morsel of food hit my lips while Melinda was present, she sneered. I passed her the sack, unsure I'd ever seen her eat.

Melinda pulled out a thickly sliced, heavily battered onion ring. The scent made my mouth water. She pushed it into her mouth and moaned.

Stella snorted. I could tell she was holding back. Melinda stunned us both by reaching back into the bag and digging out three more rings. She devoured each of them before locking eyes with me. "Didn't you bring me anything to drink?"

"Sorry, Lord Vader, but no. Just the food."

Melinda glared at Stella while she chewed another ring. "You have to have a soda with your onion rings. That's the rule."

"You have a rule about rings and pop?" I asked.

"Don't you have rules about food?" Melinda hissed. She ate another ring.

"I guess," I said. I was unsure how to broach the subject of murder, and time was half gone. Trent would return inside any minute to kick Stella and me to the curb.

"About Miss Woods." Stella ripped off the bandaid for me. "Did you kill her?"

"You are dumb, aren't you?" Melinda asked.

"Not dumb," Stella countered. "Just suspicious."

I jumped in before a fight ensued. "I don't think you had anything to do with Miss Woods's death."

"You might be the only one," Melinda said.

I leaned closer. "Why would the police suspect you?"

Melinda avoided my eyes. Instead, she glanced in the bag in search of more onion rings.

Stella said, "We don't have time. If you want our help, you'll have to spill."

"I was there," Melinda whispered.

"Where?" I asked.

"At the spa," Melinda said. "While you were being attacked."

Chapter 18

Just One Hug

"You crone!" Stella shouted. "You crusty, crone! You were there and saw Corky needed help, but you left?"

"Something like that," Melinda said.

My gut dropped. What would I have done if Melinda were being attacked?

Stella's chair squealed as she shoved away from the desk and loomed above Melinda. Gertie turned in her wheeled chair to observe.

"Calm down," I whispered to my friend. The last thing I needed was for Stella to get arrested. I wasn't sure Deadhorse would survive Melinda Carlie and Stella Michaels sharing a jail cell.

"Calm down?" Stella asked. Her eyes swelled with angry tears. "You almost died. Miss Woods did. The killer is on the loose, and Melinda could have stopped it all. Instead, she did nothing."

"I didn't do nothing," Mel argued. "I texted 911."

Stella's fists clenched. "Now, who's the dummy? You can't text 911. You have to call. They have to hear your voice and actually speak with you to send help. What did you do after you texted for help? Make a smoke signal?"

"Sit down," I pleaded with Stella.

"I called Brett," Melinda said, still struggling to save face.

The bell on the sheriff's office's front door jingled. Trent was back in the room and headed our way. Gertie watched as if we were a living soap opera. Which I guess, we sort of were.

"Time," Trent shouted as he approached.

"Not yet," Stella said.

"It's been five minutes," Trent said as he tapped his foot.

Stella turned to face down Trent, who backstepped before crossing his arms in silent fury. He despised disrespect but knew better than to push Stella.

"Come on, Corks. We're bailing."

I rose, surprised my best friend had surrendered so easily.

"You first," she said.

I squeezed between her and the desk. It was a stupid move on my part.

When Stella got mad, she made horrible choices. I should've seen her next move coming.

Gently and without hostility toward me, Stella nudged me into Melinda. Her bare shoulder was the only thing my naked hand had to grab for support. The memory flooding happened immediately.

Melinda and Brett kissing. Me crying at graduation. Melinda writing notes to Brett and passing them to him at prom. Brett passing notes back. My heart lurched in pity for my old self. This happened behind my back during what I thought was the best time of my life.

Flash forward to Mel standing in Hands-on, watching me walk into a crime scene and choosing to do nothing. These were her deep dark secrets. Why

did they revolve around me? What had
I done to her to take up root in her
thoughts?

Next came more images of Brett. Brett
kissing Miss Woods. Brett kissing me.
Brett kissing Mel. If the flash wasn't
turning my stomach, the thought of
Brett smooching other women certainly
did. I dropped my hand from Mel's
shoulder and clutched my mouth before
charging out of the office to hurl into the
bushes.

Stella shuffled along behind me. When
she noticed me catching my breath
on the curb, she plopped beside me
and took my hand in hers. Flashes
of her dreaming of murdering Melinda
rumbled across my mind. They didn't
stay long. It wasn't a buried secret
that she despised Melinda. After the

intel faded, the soft hum returned. It cooled my frazzled nerves and calmed my tumultuous stomach. I rested my head on my best friend's shoulder.

"Sorry about that," Stella said. "It was wrong of me."

"You're forgiven," I joked.

Stella chortled. "I'm a horrible friend," she began. "Melinda just makes me so mad. Both angry and crazy-wise. Then hearing her admit to ditching you... that was it. No filter left. You could've died, and she wouldn't have cared less. She may not have killed Miss Woods, but that makes her almost as guilty in my book. I thought, if you could get close, we might learn something."

"What did you expect to happen? Did you think we were going to hug?"

My second joke was more successful than the last one. Stella laughed full out. "Just one hug," she teased.

"Over my dead body," I said. Stella's laugh caught in her throat before the phrase settled over me. It nearly had been. "Thanks for caring," I whispered, letting the buzz of brown noise settle over me before releasing Stella's hand and standing.

She waited until the air blasted in the truck before asking, "What did you see?"

I snarled back at my overeager friend. "Geez, Stella. I saw myself retching into the bushes after being assaulted by my best friend."

Stella pulled away from the sheriff's department with a sideways grin. "Did you see her scarf down those onion rings?"

"Stress eating is real," I said.

"Apparently." Stella snorted. "Now, tell me everything."

I unfolded my convoluted images.

"Miss Woods and Brett? I don't think so," Stella said.

"That's what I saw," I said. "That and me walking dumbly into the quiet room."

Stella put an arm around my shoulder. Only the brown noise tickled my mind. It was refreshing. "I can't believe she did that to you."

"That's because you're my best friend. We'd die for each other."

"Yeah, we would," Stella rubbed her eyes. "We also ask each other to do the hard things." She cut the wheel and headed away from my house. Something bad was coming. I could feel it.

"Don't tell me," I whined.

"We're going to see Brett."

Chapter 19

The Ex and the Best

Brett Booker looked up from his phone as Stella ripped open the door to Fritters and Jitters and stormed up to him. "What kind of jerk..."

I grabbed her elbow before Stella could continue her tirade. "That's not how we want to start this conversation," I said.

Stella glared at Brett. "Seriously, Corks? He's eating cheesecake and playing a game on his phone. All while they suspect his girlfriend of murder."

"My fiancé," Brett said. His voice held no malice, but my teenage heart crumbled inwardly. I hadn't heard Brett and Mel were engaged.

I shot a look at Stella. Had she known and hidden it from me?

Her expression remained angry, and her face remained pointed at Brett. She hadn't known either or I would have flashed on that earlier. There was no way Stella was harboring a secret that big without feeling guilty about it. As far as I could tell, the more emotions the secret entangled, the louder it sounded.

"You expect us to say congratulations?" Stella sneered as she spoke.

I laid a hand on her arm. The gentle background hum resurfaced. No secrets needed to be spilled. "Why don't you go next door and visit the smoothie bar?

Get yourself a snack? Something that makes the jocks roll their eyes, and the homemakers swoon with envy."

"You mean the one with protein brownie bits?" Stella bit her lip as she thought. Sweets called her the way my sugar-free cold brew beckoned to me. She stayed put. "I don't want to leave you with this...."

I shook my head. "Don't," I said.

"If you're sure?"

"I've got this," I answered, waggling my suddenly magic fingers in the air. Stella would feel better knowing I would use my new gift if needed. She hugged me and left.

I helped myself to the seat across from Brett and sighed. Some pain never leaves you, and instead it morphs into your new normal. This was how Brett's deception and betrayal settled into my life.

Dating from the age of thirteen, while being the daughter of a church elder, wasn't easy, especially when you toss in everyday temptations and small-town gossip. Brett and I survived until the week of senior graduation. That's when I learned of his relationship with Mel. It stung terrible enough, but then came the fat shaming and blaming. It devastated me.

I'd wrapped up my identity in being the confident, chubby girl with a stunning boyfriend. When my confidence and boyfriend left, I became lonely, shattered, and confused.

Thankfully, Stella never left my side. She and Steve helped my heart settle, and my feet find purchase. I found a career I loved and the motivation to become healthier. It built me up more than I had been during my time with Brett.

Now just sitting across from him, I felt smaller. Until I realized it was he who was worried. Fretting his thumbs together, his anxious tell, Brett's eyes projected smugness, but his shoulders slumped in defeat.

"You know I didn't just ditch Mel," he said, as if I cared. "Her dad told me to stay out of it."

"Mel's your fiancé." I didn't choke on the words. "How are you supposed to stay out of it? Won't that make things look worse for her? Like her loved ones think she's guilty?"

Brett glanced at his phone screen. Was he waiting for a call? "That's what I asked," he said. "Her dad says I need to wait for her lawyer." Brett sniffled before downing a large gulp of iced tea. If I still knew him, it would still be minty green tea.

"That wouldn't stop me," I said. "I couldn't imagine being kept away from someone I loved when they were in crisis. I'd be sitting in the waiting room annoying the receptionist until they gave me news."

"Right," Brett said. His eyes sparked. "Stupid Trent won't even let me do that."

I flagged the barista down. No point in going through this conversation without fuel.

"Your normal?" The coffee barman asked.

I nodded.

"Sugar-free, triple shot, dark chocolate on ice coming up."

"That can't be good for you, Corks," Brett said. I was used to that phrase. I doubted it carried any real concern.

"Trent let Stella and me in," I said, with a snarky edge. Stella would be proud.

"What? Why?" Brett asked.

"We brought her lunch," I answered, avoiding bitterness.

Brett leaned forward, nearly touching my hands. I pulled them away. I needed the coffee, if only to have something to wrap my hands around. Accidental touches were a luxury I wanted to avoid.

"What were you thinking?" He asked. His anger stunned me. What had I done wrong? I'd brought his dumb fiancee lunch. Sort of. Unintentionally. He didn't know that part.

"I was being nice!"

"Nice?" He laughed. "You were rubbing it in."

The barista sat my drink down before scanning my card. The transaction gave me enough time to pause instead of tossing my frosty beverage at Brett. I'd rubbed nothing into Melinda Carlie's smug face. Though she'd flaunted her relationship with Brett, her stunningly thin body, and her supposed well-to-do status before me every time we were in the same room.

My hands stopped shaking as I sipped the first swallow of coffee. That was not a good sign. I logged away the health concern. It was time to slow my roll on my favorite beverage because it was racking up on my credit card and my health.

"I'm sorry," Brett said. He ran a hand over his perfectly groomed hair. "I know you're better than that. What were you thinking?" His voice dropped to a kinder level. "What was Trent thinking?"

"All good questions," I said.

"If they suspect Mel of killing Miss Woods, they must suspect her of trying to murder you."

"Bullseye," I said. "But I don't suspect Melinda."

"Trent's a bigger weasel than I give him credit for."

I'd thought of that too.

"How did she look?" Brett asked. His softness made my heart ache in sympathy, not longing. I let my guard down too soon. He reached out and touched me. I jolted as his innermost thoughts ambushed my brain.

Melinda berated someone. Brett shrank into the shadows as he watched Miss Woods defend herself. A female hurried up to the confrontation. Her face was fuzzy, but I knew those scrubs. It was Nurse Tunic. She grabbed Miss Woods and pulled her away from a raging Melinda before Miss Woods said another word. Brett yanked his hand away and stared at me as my stomach protested.

"Sorry," he said. He tucked his hands around his cheesecake plate. I snuggled mine around my cold plastic cup. The chilly condensation brought me out of my swirling and back to the moment. Switching sensory triggers calmed my nausea.

I ignored the obvious and asked about Miss Woods. "Why would Mel want to kill Miss Woods? What do they have on her?"

Brett scrutinized me for a moment.

"I only want to help," I assured him, but he wasn't biting. "The moment they catch who did this, I finally get to live again. I know it wasn't Mel. No way."

Brett slumped back into the booth. "Wouldn't you want her to pay for hurting you?" He asked.

Did I? Maybe. "Not like this," I said. "I want to catch whoever tried to kill me more."

It wasn't working. I wasn't convincing Brett. I leaned forward and whispered. "The man, or woman, has seen my face. They know who I am, and they know I lived. What they don't know is that I didn't see them. Until I catch them, I'm in danger, along with anyone trying to help me."

Brett's left eyebrow raised. "Why don't you let the police handle things?"

"Because they hire buttheads like Trent."

Brett chuckled. It was dark and not at all jovial, but it was a beginning. He was calming down in time for my tricky questions.

Chapter 20

Alibis and Excuses

I launched into interrogation mode with the gentlest tone I could muster. Sipping my drug of choice helped me maintain a calm facade.

"Why would the police suspect Melinda in the first place?" I asked.

Brett worried at his nail beds, avoiding eye contact with me. "You're the main reason."

"Me?" I asked, not all that shocked. "I wasn't the one that was killed. Why would Mel have something against Miss Woods?"

Again Brett averted his eyes. "There may have been a misunderstanding between Mel and me."

"About?"

Brett ignored me. I summoned my assertiveness, something I'd found after being left by Brett, and said, "If you don't speak up, how can anyone help Mel?"

"You actually want to help?" Brett asked. His baby blue eyes locked with mine, his brow furrowed in worry.

I pointed to myself. "Almost murdered. Not by Mel. Yes, I want to find who did this."

Brett rolled his shoulders and sighed. "Mel may have found text messages between me and Miss Woods."

"So?" I asked. Who cared about a text message between a mentor and an ex-student? Unless... "Oh," I said, slowly drawing unseemly conclusions.

"That's what Mel thought as well," Brett said. "I didn't know she'd been searching through my messages for weeks."

Don't roll your eyes, I told myself. It was not my business. Their relationship was not mine. I could let it be unhealthy and strained without butting in. Couldn't I? After all, they'd fought for each other and hurt people to be together. I hadn't been the only casualty.

"I know," Brett said before judgment spilled out of my mouth. "We're working on it. There you have it. Mel was stalking my texts and found a few she didn't like."

"Such as," I asked.

"An appointment with me and Miss Woods."

"An appointment?" I asked.

Brett frowned. "An appointment that Mel thought was a date."

I snorted. "You? Date Miss Woods? She's twenty years older than you. Is Melinda that insecure?"

Brett crossed his arms and glared. "If you're going to mock her, how am I supposed to believe you want to help her?"

"Sorry," I said. "Continue."

"Melinda took our texts to heart. She followed me to an appointment with Miss Woods. Here actually, at this table."

"How long ago was that?" I asked.

"Two days before the attack," Brett said. "I know it doesn't look good."

I agreed. "Can you tell me what happened?" Brett sank, and I continued pushing. "It may help."

"Okay." Brett relented with a soft growl. He was beside himself, frustrated and weary. Stella had pegged him incorrectly. Brett was frantic with fear over Melinda. Was it because she sat accused or because she was guilty?

"I promise," I whispered, though I hated taking the high road for Melinda. I wanted to be petty and cold but couldn't stomach injustice. "I won't use anything you tell me to hurt Melinda. If she's guilty, she'll be found out. I don't think that's the case. Do you?"

Brett's sideways scowl answered me. "That's what I thought."

"Okay," Brett said, leaning forward once more. He began his story in a whisper, but slowly, his voice rose as his anxiety heightened. "I was sitting here. Miss Woods was sitting where you are. She was deeply disturbed. Someone has been threatening her best friend, Mrs. Hewitt. Possibly a patient." I thought back to Mr. Hewitt's massage on the day of the attack. Were the threats on his wife knotting his shoulders? I hurried to refocus on Brett. "And yet she still came to help me."

"Help? You? How?"

Brett scowled. "Seriously, Corky, everyone needs help sometimes. You're looking at me like I'm some sort of imp. You just can't keep your feelings out of things, can you?" His jab hurt.

"Sorry," I said.

He softened. "Neither can I, but I'll try."

"Me too," I said.

"Miss Woods was helping me," Brett looked down at his cheesecake plate. "I'm thinking about becoming a therapist or counselor."

I bit my tongue. Since our long-time romance, Brett was continuously thinking of becoming something. What he was becoming was annoying. At least to me. I tried to be kind, but his constant indecision and need for my opinion proved tedious. Yet, I found it hard to turn him away.

"Wouldn't Melinda want to know about your appointment? It seems like something she might have wanted to join you in?"

Brett rolled his eyes. "She's not exactly keen on me talking to other women. She'd flip if she knew I emailed you for advice."

Rightly so, I thought and hurried to sip my drink so the words couldn't spill from my mouth.

"Mel caught us talking. She wigged out. Anyway, Miss Woods was meeting Mrs. Hewitt after our talk. Supposedly, a singles group meets here, and Mrs. Hewitt runs it. She came in right in time for Mel to end her rant. I walked out with Mel, and Mrs. Hewitt sat and consoled Miss Woods as the group members rolled in."

I frowned. That was less than helpful. What did a single's group have to do with anything? Brett's phone dinged. He jumped before hurrying to answer. After a few half-sentences, he set it into his shirt pocket and rose. I stood beside him.

"Mel's lawyer wants to see me," he said.

"That's a good sign, right?"

"I sure hope so."

"Before you go," I said. "Do you know Mel's alibi?"

Brett's brow knitted together. He still didn't believe I wanted to help. "No. She wouldn't tell me."

"She won't tell the police either," I whispered. "Maybe you can convince her to tell her lawyer."

"That's a good idea," Brett said, struggling to offer me half a grin of thanks.

Then Brett did something strange. He hugged me. Tight and close to his chest. Just like he used to when we were in high school. I couldn't help but rest my head against him for a moment.

His aftershave might have changed, but his comforting embrace was just as I remembered until the secrets began seeping into my skull.

Us kissing after the Deadhorse Canyon parade. Brett talking to Miss Woods. Him sneaking emails to me and texts to Miss Woods. Then him, kissing Mel while thinking of me. It was too much. I reeled beneath the weight of Brett's thoughts.

"What is this?" An annoyed voice approached.

I'd never been so happy to hear Steve's voice, but a whoosh of nausea overtook me before I could process it. I staggered to the nearest trash can and ralphed. My iced coffee came up as frosty as it went down.

The next thing I felt was Steve's gloved hands on my arms, leading me to Stella and their waiting blue truck.

Chapter 21

Pin up People

"What crawled up your pant leg?" Stella asked her brother, who stared out the window. "You were annoying and bubbly, and now you're...back to normal." She prodded him to get a reaction.

"Just get me back home," he said. "I have studying to do tonight."

Stella mimicked her brother in a snooty tease. Steve didn't respond. Something had him peeved. However, that was a mystery I'd have to solve later.

"Brett was meeting Miss Woods," I said.

"Like a rendezvous meeting?" Stella asked.

I shook my head. "No, they met to discuss his new career journey."

"Is there anyone Brett won't talk to?"

I crossed my arms. "Only Mel."

Steve shifted. I swear I heard him snort under his breath.

Stella turned onto her street. Once she straightened the wheel, she used one hand to count down all Brett's unseemly attributes. "He sneaks. He cheats. He left you, and he's brainless," she said. "He dates Melinda Carlie, the snobbiest snob in Deadhorse Canyon. Then, instead of running to her for help, he plagues you to affirm his life choices." She ran out of fingers before turning to her brother for help. "What do you say?"

"I say nothing," Steve said. "I want nothing to do with Brett Booker, even in conversation."

"That'll be kind of hard since he's tangled up in the case we're solving," Stella said as she pulled to the curb.

"This isn't a case," Steve said. "It's Corky's life and livelihood. Until Miss Woods's killer gets caught, Corky's in danger."

"We get that, Turbo," Stella replied. Steve slammed the truck door and sulked to his front door.

I watched him go, concerned for his well-being. "Did he not sleep enough?"

Stella shrugged. "Maybe you should touch him, and see? He was fine and then snap." Stella snapped for emphasis. "Chef Steve took over, and sweet Steve ran for the hills."

"It wasn't that bad," I said, though the shift was extreme. Especially for the always even Steve. "What was he doing at the coffee shop, anyway?"

Stella flipped the truck around and aimed it for my place. "I came and got him."

"Why?" My eyebrows rose into peaks when the idea came to me. "You got him to pull me away from Brett."

"Of course I did," she said. "Although you are determined to give Brett the benefit of the doubt, I am not nearly as generous. He's a scoundrel. And not the steamy Han Solo type. He's cruel and stupid, and...."

I opened my mouth to stop her tirade. Stella stopped herself. "I know. Enough. Anyway, I thought I might punch him if I saw him again. So, I pulled Steve away from his dumb books and brought him to rescue you."

Stella coasted into the driveway of my parent's house. She shut off the engine and gathered her purse. Before I had my belt off, she was pulling open the passenger door. That's when the questions began.

"So, Brett had a thing with Miss Woods?"

"Not a thing," I said, using one-handed quotation marks. "An appointment."

"The cops think that's enough to trigger Melinda into a murderous rage?"

I dug my keys from my pocket. "She made quite a scene."

"With witnesses?"

"A whole support group of single witnesses."

Stella's eyes glinted with mischief. "Sounds like we have a few lonely hearts to interview."

I rolled my eyes. Stella didn't notice. She charged through my front door the moment I opened it. I watched as she dug through her stash of murder board supplies and pulled out a bright red thumb tack. "So much for the paint," I whispered as I mentally counted all the pins Stella had used.

She held the scarlet pin up. "This is Mel," she said. "We'll stick her right by the entrance. Where she watched you nearly be murdered." She stabbed the pin into place.

I shook my head. "That doesn't make sense." I pointed out the flaw. "Sure, there's a window there, but the lights were out inside."

"Except for the fountain lights," Stella said.

"Light blue dim lights. They're not enough to see anything but a silhouette in the water. Especially since the lights in the entryway were still on. I turn those off last."

Stella crossed her arms. "That brat is still lying to us."

"What was she doing that was so bad?" Stella scowled.

"I'm positive it wasn't Mel."

But Stella didn't buy it. I had to dig up proof to clear Mel before my best friend let her pass. "Her fake nails would have cut me as she held me under. Wouldn't they?"

Melinda's extremely long pointed nails were a constant teasing point for me and Stella to pick on. Who wore nails that long to a massage spa? Not anyone who worked as hard as Stella and I did. Clients didn't appreciate talon marks on their skin after treatments.

Stella's shoulders slumped as she relented. "Then what is she hiding?"

"The world may never know."

Stella's nose wrinkled as she focused on her crime scene masterpiece. "Who else was there?" she asked as she pulled more pins from her stash, all with a different colored tip. She tossed a look back at me. "You and Miss Woods need no pins." Stella waved at me before I could reply.

"Mel was gone," I said. "Even if she made it to the scene as things were happening, she wouldn't have seen much."

"Surely she would've seen someone leave," Stella said.

"Unless they used the back door," I answered without thinking. I was pooped. Touching people for secrets was exhausting. I plopped onto my favorite chair.

"There is that" Stella said. "Miss Woods, Mrs. Hewitt, Davis, me," she was still listing names when I interrupted.

"Not Mrs. Hewitt. Mister. They switched places."

Stella frowned. "That's right. He'd left before you started cleaning."

"Of course," I said. "So had you."

"If only I'd waited to get coffee." Stella's eyes misted.

"Don't focus on that," I said, trying to steer the conversation back in the right direction. "Who else was at the spa that evening?"

"Tucker," Stella held up a pin. "Mrs. Cockle." She scratched her head. "Mel would know, but I'm not asking her."

I yawned and stretched. "She may remember, but her book is in the spa. She wouldn't be able to double-check."

"She'd remember," Stella pouted. "She remembers everything in that book of hers."

That's when I remembered. "No, the page from that day was ripped out."

"What?"

I sat up straighter. "Yes, she blamed us for tearing it out. All I did was adjust the Hewitt's names."

"Someone must have taken it after that."

"Does it matter?"

What I was concerned about wasn't the client sheet. It was the picture of the spilled potted plant at the corner of the quiet room and entryway. The scattered earth hosted three footprints. All of them headed away from the front door and to the treatment rooms.

"Whoever the killer is," I whispered as I thought. "They didn't leave through the front door."

Chapter 22

Two Doctors

The next morning I was up and dressed before Stella. She slept on my couch, beneath the crime scene photos. I had a doctor's appointment to attend. Not to mention, I wanted to see the Hewitts. Perhaps one of them saw something odd on the day of the attack.

I tiptoed through the living room as Stella drooled. One false eyelash stuck to the side of her cheek. It fluttered at me as the air conditioner kicked on. I opened the fridge, using the new sound to muffle my movements. Waking Stella had many disadvantages. She was not a morning person. Plus, she'd want to ride along to the appointment. That meant she'd need to dress, and Stella was an extremely slow primper. I'd be late if I wasn't careful.

I snatched a protein shake and used one of Stella's hot pink sticky pads notes to leave her a message. Then, I sneaked out of my house, locking the door after me. I nearly spat my shake on my mother's shirt when I noticed her lounging in my front porch rocker.

"You nearly killed me!"

Mom struggled not to snicker. "I'm sorry, Baby. I didn't want you to walk to the car without me. Strange things have been happening around here. I didn't want to risk it."

I straightened and forced a smile to my face. "I know," I whispered. "Thanks."

Mom stood and led me to the family car, a hatchback hybrid. I could drive it when I wanted, but my feet were my favorite way to get around. However, the doctor's office was a few miles outside my normal walking radius.

"What strange things have I missed this morning?" I asked as I slid into the passenger seat.

"Only that they released Melinda Carlie." Mom grimaced as she spoke.

"She didn't do anything. They should release her."

Mom's frown tightened. "After all those things she said about you, they should want to keep you safer than letting a bitter bean like Melinda loose."

My lips curved into a half smile on my lips. "I love you Mom," I said as I squeezed her hand. "Mel's innocent."

My mother blew a raspberry as she turned onto the highway. "Maybe of hurting Miss Woods but not of hurting you."

"Even of that," I said. "She didn't harm anyone. Not this time."

Mom settled with my last statement. She was on Team Stella in wanting Melinda out of my life forever. I wonder if she doubted Melinda had a single redeeming quality in her bones.

I allowed the topic to drop. Melinda's release meant the police finally had her alibi. Perhaps they'd start searching for the actual killer now. That was good news to me. I wanted my life back, small as it appeared from the outside looking in.

Mom talked about her scrapbooking club as she pulled into the medical office parking lot. She was still chatting about it when we rode the elevator to the third floor until Mrs. Hewitt entered the car.

"Corky," Mrs. Hewitt cooed. She offered me a soft smile before pressing the button for the fourth floor. "I'm glad to see you out and about. Are you here for a check-up?"

Mom, in her mom's way, answered for me. "Exactly right."

Mrs. Hewitt looked me over. "You look strong enough. Anything else going on?"

I shrugged. I wasn't about to tell her about my magic fingers.

"Why don't you come up and see me after you're done with your appointment?" The offer was kind, but I couldn't afford a therapy appointment on top of a regular check-in. "Seriously, you need to talk. Come on up. It's a paperwork day for me. I'll take a break, and we'll chat. No fee, no notetaking, just talk."

Mom nudged me so hard that I nearly fell into the elevator doors. Lucky for me, they were opening. "Okay," I answered. "Thanks."

I heard Mom thanking Mrs. Hewitt, but once the kind therapist rested her hand on my unprotected forearm, theirs wasn't the loudest conversation happening.

Instead, Mrs. Hewitt paced in front of her paperwork. She argued with someone on the phone. "I can't do that," she said. "Not without proof." She clicked a red pen before writing the name Brandon on a yellow legal pad. "We can't ruin someone's reputation on rumors."

Then snap! I was back in the elevator. "You okay?" Mom asked me as the elevator doors closed. I couldn't remember separating from Mrs. Hewitt's reassuring touch.

The hall fuzzed and spun. I blinked away nausea. It would not do, upchucking right before seeing the doctor. He'd put me back in the hospital if he figured out why I was sick. Mom led me to the office waiting room—her hand in mine. The gentle buzz soothed my swirling stomach. I sat beside her, regaining my balance until the doctor called me into his office.

I had flashlight beams stabbed in my eyes. My ears, nose, and throat were checked. I walked a straight line and stood on one leg. It wasn't until the doctor inspected my head that our skin brushed together. My doctor was easy. His guilty pleasure was a double bacon cheeseburger on Fridays. He hoped his nutrition-centered wife would never find out. My stomach still spiraled with the contact, but his easygoing nature kept me from succumbing to it.

My impromptu visit with Mrs. Hewitt was an entirely different story.

Chapter 23
Sponging Secrets

"Don't go in there," My mom hollered behind me as I dashed into Mrs. Hewitt's office. The front door to her suite was ajar. I supposed for me. When I walked in, I knew better. Someone had trashed the place. If movies meant anything, it didn't appear they were looking for anything in particular. They were ticked and raging.

 "Mrs. Hewitt!" I yelled as I entered her private office. At first, the room appeared empty. Then I saw her feet. I hurried to her side. My mother, still in the waiting area, was talking on the phone, calling for help.

"Mrs. Hewitt," I whispered, pleading with her to be okay. A small stream of sticky blood dribbled from a cut on her forehead. I cringed as I reached for the therapist's hand. Memories racked me, but not before I registered a pulse.

Threats and fear rippled through Mrs. Hewitt's heart. A week of terror mingled with grief followed a month of looking behind her shoulder. She'd liked Miss Woods and had warned her.

"About what?" I asked the unconscious woman.

Her memories answered with flashes of slashed tires and broken windows. A hand-scrawled note rested beside her phone on her desk. I tried glancing up toward the spot I figured I'd find the note, but my vision was blurry, mingled with Mrs. Hewitt's thoughts.

Next came pictures of Miss Woods, crying as a younger woman berated her. Only the woman's profile came into the viewscreen of my mind. Her blonde curly hair masked the rest of her face as she pointed fingers at Miss Woods and yelled words I couldn't make out.

Behind Miss Woods's left shoulder, stood a man I'd recognize anywhere. Tucker Williams, a cowboy charmer and a frequent client of the Hands-On Healing Spa. I squinted, mentally and physically, to draw out his expression. When I thought I had it and Mrs. Hewitt's memory cleared, hands ripped me back from the therapist's side.

Mom held me in a worrisome hug, and her buzzing transparency soothed my spinning stomach. My frayed nerves were beyond overwhelmed. Someone wanted Miss Woods dead and had lived out that want. Was it the same woman Mrs. Hewitt watched bully her friend? Had that woman later turned on the spectator of the attack? Did that mean Tucker was next?

Mom rattled on as we awaited questioning and continued during our drive home. She struggled to distract me, as if that would save me from reliving my attack or stop me from replaying the scene at the office. I kept resetting the room.

The medics forced me out before I could examine Mrs. Hewitt's desk, but I caught sight of a stack of legal pads. There was one with the letter B, hastily written in red. Did the B stand for Brandon?

I sat silently pondering Mrs. Hewitt's thoughts as my mother drove home. I couldn't shake the feeling of dread that had passed from Mrs. Hewitt's mind to mine. Though my mother never stopped scanning me for injury and insanity I couldn't break the quiet. How could I explain what was happening to me and to my small town?

In the driveway, Mom shut off the engine and sighed. She wrapped me in a bear hug. Her concern washed over me like the central air had just kicked on. I let it flow through me until her thoughts faded into a neutral hum. She let me go to pray aloud over me. I relished the encouragement. Life was growing heavy around me.

"I'll see you later," I told my mother, who was reluctant to let me leave her presence. She moseyed along beside me to my backyard cottage, and I didn't blame her. We'd been through a lot that day, and it wasn't noon yet. However, if she didn't let me go her brown noise hugs might erase my newest whispers. I had to get to Stella and spill the memories before they disappeared. I unlocked my front door after my mom turned toward the main house.

Stella nearly jumped as I crossed the threshold of my tiny house. "You couldn't wake me?" she asked instead of a greeting. I shut the door behind me and locked it.

"No time," I said sternly, but Stella took it badly.

"You didn't have time to rouse me? I could've been ready and with you at the doctor's in a flash."

I groaned. "First, you are not that easy to wake. Second, you are the slowest dresser in the world, and third, that's not what I'm talking about."

Stella shot upright and smiled. "You sponged someone's secrets, didn't you?" She scrambled for a notepad and pen. With a click, she was ready. I told her everything I could remember.

"You see the connection, don't you?"

I shook my head. "It's too new for me to process."

Stella's eyes twinkled with cunning. "They were all at the spa."

"Who was?"

"Miss Woods, Mrs. Hewitt, and Tucker Williams. They were all there just a few hours before the murder." Stella wrote each name on a sticky note and slammed it onto my living room wall-turned murder board. "Miss Woods was receiving treatment after Tucker had just finished. Mrs. Hewitt was switching places with her husband. They were all there."

"Are you saying Tucker is the killer? Because I thought you were still hung up on Melinda?"

Stella waved a hand at the thought. "I just hoped she'd dangle a little longer, that's all. Besides, she's not completely off the hook. She was there, too."

"Okay," I said with a clap. "Let's list everyone who would have been at the spa that day."

"That's called opportunity. Did they have opportunity?"

I crossed my arms. "I don't care what it's called. Let's move along."

"Secret sponging makes someone grumpy."

"You try it sometime." I stuck out my tongue.

"If only," Stella snuck in her last word before beginning the list of suspects again. "Miss Woods, Melinda, Mr. Hewitt, Mrs. Hewit from earlier, Tucker from earlier, Davis, you, me, and Misty Cloke."

"Misty? I didn't see her there."

"You were busy with Mr. Hewitt. She popped in to buy a gift card. I know because Melinda had me handle the transaction."

"And you just remembered right now?"

Stella blinked as my voice rose. "It's been a wild week."

"But don't you see? Misty has blonde curly hair."

"And?"

"In my vision, so did the lady threatening Mrs. Hewitt."

"Where are we supposed to find Misty?" Stella asked. "The spa is closed. There's no reason for us to call her."

I looked toward the ceiling in concentration. "My bet is she'll be wherever Tucker is."

Stella's eyes rounded as she whipped out her phone. She scrolled before turning the screen to face me. "I looked this up, after you visited with Brett."

It was a social media page for Fritters and Jitters. Front and center on her screen was a virtual bulletin board announcing the singles group from Brett's memory banks. Tucker Williams and Miss Woods were smiling in the advertisement. As luck would have it, the group met later that evening. So much for a decompressing afternoon with Stella.

"Mrs. Hewitt won't make it," I said. There was no way the therapist would keep her appointment, leading the group.

"I'm guessing her buddy, Nurse Tunic, will take her place. Someone must explain to the group why their coach can't be there."

"So, we hope we bump into Tucker and Misty."

Stella shrugged. "If not, we can always probe Nurse Tunic about their connection to Miss Woods."

Again, Stella's plans left a knot in my stomach.

Chapter 24

One Not So Lonely Heart

The day drifted past, then all at once, it was time to get ready. I watched as Stella swiped a perfect wing of liner on her lids moments before my mother burst into the cottage.

"You really should keep your door locked," she said, panic smeared across her face.

I wrapped my arms around her. "Hey, Momma," I said, sounding cheerful and not crime-obsessed.

"Don't hey me," she said. I could tell she was not falling for it. "What in the world is going on in your living room?"

Stella rolled her eyes but didn't stop applying her makeup. "Just doing a little closure therapy." It wasn't untrue. I was certain finding the killer and my attacker would bring me closure. However, my mom was sharp and would not take an answer that bland at face value.

"By hashing up the scene of the crime?" Mom's voice rose.

"We've got to find out who did this, Momma," I said.

Mom's skin prickled against mine as she held my hand. Thoughts of worry invaded my brain. I could sense the intense fight of fear and pride in my mother's mind. "The police are doing that," she said. Her tone fell flat, but she knew as well as we did that Trent wasn't the sort of officer to go out of his way. Until our regular sheriff returned to town, we were mostly on our own.

"We're being careful," I said.

Mom dropped my hand and glared into my eyes. "Visiting Melinda Carlie is not being careful. Karting yourself around town in all black in summer is not being careful. Barreling into a looted office is not being careful. You're being reckless."

With that, she shoved a large plastic bag into my arms. I followed her as she stormed into the living room and stared at the crime wall. Tears silently clustered in her eyes as she pointed to the wall. "That's my baby up there," she said. "When Stella called me, my knees buckled in terror. I never want to feel that fear ever again. Ever."

I sank. I couldn't hurt my mom, especially knowing what I now knew. She needed me. I was about to say I would end the hunt, even if Stella would be disappointed. Then my mother shocked me.

She squinted at the board and back at me. "You get the monster who did this," she said. "Just don't become one."

Her tears flowed as she hugged me tightly. I stood there in the soft hum of honesty for a while. Stella's impatience didn't hinder the moment. I allowed mom as long as she needed to find her bearings. She pulled away and swiped at her eyes.

"Promise you'll ask for help," she said. "None of this, running into dark places alone."

I nodded.

"Then I'll stay by my phone and keep praying. Text me when you move from place to place. I can send backup if you need it," she said, then kissed my cheek. She nodded toward the bundle in my hand. "That's from the hospital. We forgot the rest of your belongings."

The bag crinkled as I opened it. "Don't the police need this?"

"Trent," Stella and Mom muttered in frustration.

"We'll be at Fritters if you need us, Mrs. Hobbs," Stella said.

"Got it. Keep me posted," Mom answered before squeezing me one last time and heading out the door. She didn't tell me she loved me, which was odd. Then again, so was the entire situation.

I dropped the hospital bag on my reading chair and locked the door. Even though Stella and I were nearly ready to leave, knowing that had been unlocked sent chills up my neck.

Stella nodded at me as if she was resetting the moment. Mom was gone. Now, it was time to move on. She hurried back to my vanity mirror and finished her makeup.

"Why are you getting so dolled up?" I asked. "It's not like you're joining the singles group."

Stella popped her gum. Her eyes twinkled with mischief. "You never know. Maybe I will. Plus Tucker Williams will be there. He only ever sees me at work so maybe I can get him to look my way."

I groaned. "He's already with Misty, remember?"

"Your secret senses picked up a fight. I doubt they're still together," Stella said before layering on lip gloss. "And don't mention the age thing. He's far from being a silver fox, but give him another twenty years."

Ignoring my always-love-pinning friend, I twisted my hair into a semi-decent bun. "All I want is another cold brew," I said.

"Maybe make it a decaf," Stella suggested. "You're getting jumpy."

"Avoiding death isn't a good enough reason to be on edge?"

Stella snagged her purse in one hand and held my shoulder with the other. "C'mon, Corks, let's make this as fun as possible."

She drove us to Fritters while acting out how she planned to woo Tucker Williams during their "interview" session. I sunk low in the seat. Stella's love matches never worked out the way she envisioned them. Still, I gave her five stars for perseverance.

My mouth watered as the scent of caffeinated delights smacked my senses. Stella held open the door, allowing me to enter ahead of her. What I assumed to be the singles group, huddled near the back of the shop. Stella boldly approached the group.

Tucker Williams smiled when he spotted us. "Well, if it isn't my spa ladies. Don't tell me you're both joining our little group?"

Misty Cloke stood beside Tucker flashing dagger eyes at Stella, who pretended not to notice. "We might," Stella said.

"You picked a horrible time to show up," Misty said, sullen and sulky. "Mrs. Hewitt had an accident."

I blinked at the term accident. What I stumbled upon was anything but an accident.

"We heard," Stella said, leaving my discovery out of the conversation.

That's when Nurse Tunic turned around to face us.

She smiled at me, but I cringed as I knew what came next. "Miss Hobbs," she said. "You should be resting. So much has happened with your head and you finding Valerie today."

Misty's eyes bugged. She was shocked, and a bit aggravated. Tucker Williams was a different story. His eyes flickered with a feeling I couldn't understand.

"You found her?" Misty asked frustration in her tone.

I didn't bother replying. Stella did it for me. "She was going in for a checkup and stumbled upon Mrs. Hewitt. Someone tossed the poor woman's office and then clobbered her on the head."

"Like what happened to you?" Misty asked.

I pulled back inwardly before saying, "Worse."

"I doubt that" Tucker said. "But look at you braving the world already."

Nurse Tunic frowned at Tucker's strange encouragement. Misty scowled at me and then at Stella.

Misty pushed her way through the rest of the group and pulled her purse from the back of the chair. "Since there's no meeting," she said. "I'm out of here."

I watched as our lead suspect glared at Tucker Williams. "Coming?" she asked the tall cowboy.

Tucker waffled a moment before turning to Misty. "Yes, ma'am."

Then, in typical Stella fashion, my bestie grabbed my wrist and stuck it on Misty's hand as it reached Tuckers. Two paths of thought attacked me at once. They fluttered in like Junebugs, bumping into one another. I couldn't collect them fast enough to put them where they belonged.

I sank into the chair Misty's purse had rested on as the swift connection broke.

"What are you thinking!" Misty hollered at Stella.

I'd love to know the answer to that one, I thought as my head flurried.

"You can't just waltz in here and take over the group," Misty spat.

Stella struggled to calm her. "We were just here to get coffee."

"Sure, you were," Misty yelled. "You just came over and said hi like your friend stumbled upon two attacked people. It's all one big coincidence."

I rested my forehead on the palms of my hands as the flashes fell into place. The noise wasn't helpful. I really needed a fully charged cold brew.

Chapter 25

Back to the Board

"That was a disaster," I told Stella as I flopped onto my couch. "We weren't there ten minutes before you ticked off our primary suspect. I should say, ex-main suspect."

Stella was about to argue, but she caught my last words before she let hers fly. "What did you see?"

I rubbed my temples and sipped my extra-large beverage. "Just that Misty Cloke has a major thing for Tucker."

"Everyone knows that. He's the one she bought the gift certificate for. A couple's massage."

I shuddered. "Maybe she should have made it a group package. Tucker is 'dating' every woman in the group."

"What?" Stella giggled as she took a seat near my ankles.

"And not just in this group," I said.

"What a player," Stella smirked. "Was he dating Miss Woods?"

I replayed the flashes of past dates in my head. The one thing Tucker Williams wanted to keep under his hat was his love of the ladies. It came across the most vividly as I soaked in his secrets. Misty's extreme jealousy came up next.

"He dated her," I said. "I don't think they hit it off."

Stella kicked off her sandals and tucked her feet onto the couch. My air conditioner churned to life, freezing the summer sweat to my skin as I lounged.

"Spill everything," Stella demanded.

"First and most important. Misty didn't kill anyone. She was sure mad enough to, but she wasn't in town."

"How do you know that?"

I tapped my temple. "Her big secret, other than being madly in love with Tucker, is that she's not a natural blonde. After picking up the gift card, she was getting her roots done two towns over."

Stella bent over laughing. "That was a huge bust. From all angles."

I paused to text my mom and let her know we'd made it home safely.

"Well, it's back to the board then," Stella said with a clap. "Thank goodness, Chef Steve has a final coming up. He's making us dinner and will bring it over later."

"Great," I said. "But where do we look now? Misty's a no-go. Tucker may have a secret to hide, but he's sort of proud of it, not worried it will spill."

"It circles back to Mel being jealous of Miss Woods and you," Stella answered. I opened my mouth to speak, but Stella shushed me with a raised hand. "I know. She has an unspoken alibi. Too bad your magic fingers couldn't find it."

I turned to face the wall. "It's got to be here," I said.

Stella frowned. "Unless someone walks in from the street, it's just us and the customers. No one else had access."

"Could someone have walked in without me noticing?" I asked. Someone had trampled on the spilled plant soil after I'd spilled it.

Stella stood before her monstrosity murder board. "I would have seen them leave."

"Except you weren't looking for them. Although, if Mel was there, she must've seen someone leave."

Stella put her hands on her hips, her brows furrowing in deep concentration. "That means they left through the back door. There's no way, while texting for help, she didn't notice anyone leave the spa."

"Except she wasn't there when you pulled up," I pointed out. "You didn't see her."

My friend shrugged off her anger at Melinda Carlie and thought aloud. "Perhaps she was in her car. It was still in her spot."

"That still rules out escaping from the front," I said.

"Does that mean your attacker was still in the spa when I came in?" Stella's face paled at the thought. It was a possibility. "They left as I was helping you out of the pond, but before the police arrived."

"It seems like it," I answered.

Stella paced the width of the couch. The hem of her jeans flapped along in stride, creating a breeze that rattled the clear plastic hospital bag. It wiggled on the coffee table. I grabbed it before it fell into Stella's path.

"What's that?"

I cracked open the bag. "It's what I had on me during my attack, I guess."

"Wouldn't the police need that?"

I shrugged. "Maybe they already looked at it?" With a new focus, Stella sat on the floor beside me, awaiting the reveal. I rifled through the contents. "Honestly, it's just my working scrubs and shoes."

My finger flicked against a small hard object. I couldn't fathom what it could be. Pinching it, I pulled the comma-shaped bud from the bag and wilted.

"It's Miss Woods's," I said, holding the earbud. "It must've been lodged in my hair," I recalled its lazy spiraling as I was held beneath the water.

Stella pulled a long sheet from the bag and read it. "The inventory sheet says there's only one in the bunch."

"She must've been wearing her other one. This one fell out during her attack." I was racked by the mental image of the savage's perseverance, giving me guilty shivers. I tossed the bud across the room. Stella hastily retrieved it.

"Poor Miss Woods loved her romance novels and podcasts. It's a shame she never found her soulmate," Stella said. She inspected the rose gold bud. "Do you think it has the killer's fingerprints on it?" Her voice raised in excitement.

I slowly shook my head. "If it did, they're long gone by now. There's no telling how many nurses or emergency techs touched that thing before they put it in my bag."

"What are you going to do with it?" Stella asked.

"I guess give it back to Miss Woods," I answered. I'm sorry the exchange wouldn't be face-to-face at the spa.

"I'll go with you," Stella said.

Just then, the front door opened. Stella failed to lock it once again. Steve entered carrying a platter mummified in plastic wrap. "Go where?" he asked as he set down the dinner dishes.

"To the cemetery," I answered. "Pay private respects to Miss Woods."

Steve's smiling face fell into somberness before he uncovered his masterpieces. "I didn't have time to make anything special. Just quinoa with mango salsa and pulled pork sliders."

My stomach rumbled in gratitude.

Chapter 26
Church Ladies

Sunday morning church was uncomfortable. One reason was because I wanted to continue the hunt for my attacker but didn't know where to start. Next was the constant neck craning of the church members before me. As my first major social outing since the graveside service, the populace seemed overly curious about my well-being. I felt sorry for the preacher between them staring at me and then flashing attention toward Melinda. His message had to fight for purchase with the crowd.

Meanwhile, I sunk low in the pew and hid behind my mother's shoulder. I coward, like Little Corky would do, as the sermon continued. Mom patted my knee as she used to when I was in pigtails. The preacher wasn't long-winded, but unfortunately, the church ladies were circling.

Three women from my mom's bunco group swarmed at the final amen. They pawed and fussed over me. The physical contact would have been tiresome on its own, but with my new secret sifting talents, it was excruciating. I couldn't tell whose thoughts were whose. The memories and thoughts pummeled me.

Mom caught the tension and did her best to thwart her friends. Even her mild-mannered reprimands didn't stave them off. After giving it her best shot, she handed me over to Stella, who arrived by my side just in time for the onslaught.

"Take her home quick," Mom commanded.

"You got it, boss," Stella said, whistling for Steve.

I was seconds away from vomiting when we arrived at their truck. Stella hugged me, allowing her buzz to soothe my pounding head. We jetted toward home before the church ladies left the building.

I rested my head on Stella's shoulder as Steve drove me home. "They're all worried," I told them, remembering the main thread of the group's flashes.

"That only makes sense. We're all worried," Steve said as he turned onto the main drive.

"What else did they say?" Stella asked, eager to see if my new gift was churning up leads. Lucky for her, I heard something else.

"They're all talking about a murder that happened ten years back. They said it was the last one in Deadhorse Canyon until Miss Woods."

Steve's brow furrowed. "Wouldn't we have heard about that?"

Stella waved a hand in dismissal. "We were junior high twerps. It would have flown over our heads if we had." She turned her head as I sat up straight. "Did they tell you who was murdered?"

"Nope," I answered. "Only that it was tragic, and they passed away before their time."

"We'll look it up when we get back to your place," Stella said. "Then, if you still want to head to the cemetery, we can."

I shrugged. "I'm not sure I'm up for it after the group hug." Just then, my phone trilled in my pocket, as did Stella's. "Group text?"

Stella was quick on the draw. "It's Mel," she sneered. "She says she has our paychecks and will meet everyone at the spa."

Steve asked what I was thinking. "Is the spa open?"

"I'm not sure I'm ready to confront the spa," I said.

Stella placed a reassuring hand on my shoulder. "That's probably why she wants to meet there," Stella said. "But have no fear. She says we're meeting out front. However, she'll be there for the next thirty minutes only."

"What a tender heart," Steve mocked. "So glad she's willing to do that. Since it is her job and all."

Stella elbowed her brother in agreement. Her smile was warming but I couldn't stop the chills dancing along my arm hair. I didn't want to go back to the crime scene. Having it displayed on my wall was bad enough. Hanging out at the location might drive me over the edge.

"Don't worry," Stella said. "I'll be there."

"So will I," Steve said. "There's no way I'm leaving you alone with Mel or butthead Brett."

Stella turned a quizzical eye toward her big brother. He ignored her and u-turned past my house. It was normal for the Michaels to join my family for lunch after church.

No doubt Steve would spruce up whatever mom had simmering in the crock-pot. No matter how comforting mom's food promised to be, I wasn't sure I'd be able to stomach the meal knowing what lay ahead for me. However, her meal would need to wait for a bit longer.

Then Stella added with a giggle, "Maybe this time you'll have the nerve to touch Mel and find out her alibi. Hopefully, it's embarrassing as all get out."

Chapter 27

Payday

Melinda's smug expression followed the truck as we pulled into the spa parking lot, and it backfired for emphasis. She laughed and nudged Brett with her elbow. I cringed while struggling to keep my face from showing my distrust.

"Want me to wait in the car?" Steve asked.

Stella nodded. "We don't need you getting confrontational with Brett Booker. Not today. Besides, Davis is here. He'll protect us." Stella pointed out the windshield as Davis Pile waved at us.

"I remember Davis," Steve said. "Slightly. I wonder what brought him back to Deadhorse Canyon?"

I scooted out of the front seat and held the door open for Stella, who turned back to her brother. "I'm sure you can ask him later. As for now, I want to get my check and get away from Melinda. Besides, we still have a murder to solve."

Steve rolled his eyes. It amazed me how much the brother and sister looked alike when they were throwing sour attitudes around.

I leaned into Stella and whispered. "I didn't know Davis was from around here."

"Yeah," Stella said. "I didn't know that either until he told me at the gravesite."

"Weird conversation for a cemetery," I said. Stella led the way up to Melinda, who ignored us.

"Not really," she said. "He was paying his respects to a classmate before Miss Woods's memorial took place."

"How are you holding up?" Davis asked. He strolled up right after we'd finished discussing him. I stared at him blankly. "Your head?" Davis pointed to my temple. The heat from his hand sent my secret senses off. I pulled away, trying to keep a smile on my face. I didn't want to hurt Davis's feelings, but I really didn't want to be touched again.

"I'm good," I said, my voice shaking. "At least, I think I am."

Davis crossed his arms and surveyed me. "You sure?" he asked. "Maybe you need a massage. I'm available for you if you need a session."

The thought made my palms sweat. I couldn't imagine an hour of skin-to-skin contact. What kind of emotional rollercoaster would that be? I went to thank Davis when Melinda interrupted by thrusting an envelope in Davis's face.

"The boss says," Melinda referred to Hands-On's owner. "There's a large bonus for anyone willing to help with cleaning up once the police let us back in. Can I count on you?" I couldn't help but notice that she talked only to Davis and not to me.

"I've got to make money somehow," Davis said, without hesitation.

"Great, I'll text you when we get the green light," Melinda said, leaving me out of the offer. I didn't want to clean up a crime scene, anyway.

"Here's your check," Melinda said. She flipped a white envelope at me, twirling it with her fingers. Davis fell for her theatrics and reached out for it. I overreacted and did the same. Our three hands all grabbed each other as they grabbed the envelope. Thoughts collided upon me.

"It was bad enough before. Then she had to get skinny," Melinda's thoughts probed me. I looked past her thoughts to catch her expression. She glared at me as if she noticed my eavesdropping. Then with a slow blink, she let go of my hand.

Davis was still attached to me. He stood staring at a tombstone, blank and stoic. "Death had that effect on many people.

She's shut down the feelings before they get too intense to handle," his thought whispered. He, too, stared at me as if he knew I could see through him. Putting my check into my hand as I shuddered, he squinted at me as if trying to figure me out.

I held back my shock. Instead, I focused on the snarky exchange happening between Melinda and Stella. The nausea faded in time to hear Melinda toss verbal daggers at my best friend.

Stella was quick to respond. "Oh yeah," she said with a hand on her hip. "Then why don't you tell us why you keep hiding your alibi? Even lying about seeing Corky's attack. Just to deflect your sordid story."

Even though Stella and I had decided that it would have been impossible for

Melinda to witness my attack and the killer, it didn't mean she wasn't there. Stella was fishing. When she spotted me watching her dramatics, she winked. I knew what she wanted but didn't want to do it. I didn't want to touch Melinda Carlie again. Her thoughts mocked and confused me all at once. Stella double winked.

"Excuse me," I told Davis, who was still squinting at me. Summoning up my courage and hoping for thick skin, I approached the battling duo.

I placed a hand on Melinda's shoulder just as Stella asked her again for her alibi. The evidence surfaced in a flurry of anger and embarrassment. Melinda pulled away from me a nanosecond after contact, but it was too late. I'd found the answer to Stella's question.

"Do you two weirdos mind? I'm doing a job here," Mel snorted and sidestepped away. Brett shot me a sad, sympathetic glance. I didn't return the sentiment. A frown settled on his handsome face at my lack of response.

"See you later, Davis," I said as I passed Mr. Pile.

Stella scooted in by Steve, who gave us both the stink eye as I slid into the seat beside her.

"What was all that about?" He asked. There was no use playing innocent. He knew I'd been using my talent on Melinda. I wouldn't have touched the woman otherwise.

"Corky's trying to figure out what Melinda's alibi is. Since she'd been so stealthy about it, we returned the favor," Stella said with a snicker in her tone.

"I understand her." Steve referenced, regarding his kid sister. "But you Corks? You're better than that."

"You want the murder solved, don't you?" Stella asked, her voice raising in angst. She didn't give Steve a moment to answer. "This is how we have to do it."

"By invading other people's privacy?"

I cringed. Was that what I was doing? I was ashamed of myself. What was I becoming a superhero or villain?

"Just this once, Steve," I said.

Stella growled. "No, not just this once. As often as we need to. It's not something she can turn off."

"Yet," Steve said. "But she can wear these." He lifted his pleather-gloved hands in a demonstration.

"Yes, and she can look just as freaky as you do." Stella locked her arms across her chest and pouted. "Corky's got a good reason for using her gift."

Steve disapproved. His adamant dislike marred his boyish face.

"I didn't need to know Melinda's alibi. I could've trusted the police, but she made me so mad I could nearly spit."

"And there's the truth," he said. "Finally."

"Spill," Stella said, ignoring her brother. "What's Mel's alibi?"

Guilt washed over me. "She was seeing a doctor," I said without expounding.

"Then why didn't she just say so," Steve asked.

I didn't dare tell him. But without a word, Stella clued into my silence. "She's having work done."

"Work?" Stella gave Steve a look that would peel paint until he, too, clued in. "That's her business."

"Yes, it is," I agreed.

Stella couldn't sit still with the new clue. "Why on earth would Melinda the looker want or need work done?"

Ignoring the question, as Steve drove us back to lunch wasn't easy. Stella glared at me the entire drive. However, I was keeping that little fact to myself because Brett and I were the reason. Melinda was insanely jealous and worried that Brett Booker was one impetuous moment away from running back to me.

Chapter 28
Time to Sift

Mom's chicken casserole with cauliflower rice was scrumptious—perfect comfort food for a week of stress. I allowed myself to eat two plates, even though seconds weren't on my eating plan. The double helping was sure to place me in food drowsiness. After my strange emotional reveal from Melinda about Brett and me, I wanted a quiet nap to distract myself. I hoped the pause would do me well.

But Stella wasn't having it. She dove into conversation with my folks and grilled them without mercy. Thank goodness she'd been around long enough for my parents to understand her whims almost as much as I did.

"The ladies at church," Stella said. I wondered how she would phrase my ability to see into the ladies' thoughts. My mother wasn't privy to my new gift. Mostly because I hoped it would go away. But also, how was I supposed to tell her I could see people's thoughts and secrets? I listened as Stella continued. "They mentioned something about a murder a few years back."

Mom recoiled. Dad choked on his tea. "I remember that," he said without adding detail. "First murder in almost twenty years."

Stella would be hard-pressed getting more of a response from my dad.

My mom was the one to pump for information.

"They didn't categorize it as a murder," Mom added. "It was a suspicious death."

"Suspicious death?" Steve asked. "What's the difference?"

"One can be proved to be malicious. The other might have been an accident."

"Who died?" Stella asked.

Mom's face fell as she tracked down the memory. "A senior from the high school. The day after prom, if I remember it correctly."

I was sure Mom was right, mostly because she usually got her facts straight.

Dad piped in between bites. "Drowned in the town fountain." I shivered, but not before realizing Mom had kicked Dad from under the table.

"Sorry, Honey," Dad said.

I tried to smile.

Steve chimed in. "I think I remember that" he said. "I heard the guy parkoured himself to death. Slammed his head against the side of the fountain before sliding under."

Mom reached out to me, striving to bring comfort to a triggering conversation. I offered her a smile and hoped it would ease both of our anxieties.

"Parkour?" Dad asked.

"Extreme stunts and stuff," Mom said. It was a good answer.

"Meaning he back flipped himself to death?" Dad took another bite of the casserole after asking his last question.

Steve answered. "Something like that."

"They weren't sure?" Stella asked. "What made the police unsure?"

Mom retrieved her hand from mine and threaded her fingers together. "There was evidence that he wasn't alone. Police think a friend saw what happened but was too spooked to call for help. Possibly because they were drinking."

"That's awful," I said.

"It devastated the family," Mom added. "They moved from Deadhorse Canyon before the school year ended, leaving their house empty. It has been for years. Until recently."

"Recently?" Stella asked.

"A brother or something moved back to town recently. Rumor is he's going to flip the place."

Stella patted her mouth with a napkin. "Was there any investigation?"

Mom shrugged. "I would assume so. Steve might remember better. It was while you were in Deadhorse Canyon High."

Steve blinked when all eyes turned toward him. "What year?" he asked, buying time to collect his response.

"The year Braiden Daze won some national something or other. It was plastered all over the town, even before he died."

I choked on my iced tea. "Braiden?"

Mom nodded. "Or Brandon?"

Steve sighed as he concentrated. "I remember those posters. It was my freshman year."

"Sounds right," Mom said. She shoved away from the table and began collecting finished plates.

"What do you remember about Brandon?" Stella asked.

I listened intently. Visions of the name Brandon flashed in my mind. What linked Mrs. Hewitt and Miss Woods to Brandon Daze? That is, if he was the correct Brandon.

Steve handed my mother his plate and thanked her before responding. "Not much. Just that he was not the all-around nice kid the town likes to remember he was. I think I remember there being a group of anti-Brandons at school. I stayed out of it."

"You stayed out of everything," Stella mumbled.

"Would the Daze family have had reason to visit with the Hewitts?" I asked dumbly.

"I think a death in the family is a noble reason to visit a counselor," Stella said.

I rolled my eyes at her. "I mean before that."

Steve shrugged. "I don't know about them, but rumor had it plenty of Brandon's marks were in counseling."

Mom replaced the casserole dish with a pan of frozen yogurt key lime pie. My sugar senses sounded. Mom then set a smaller tin in front of me. "No sugar added," she said, motioning to my tiny pie. "High school rumors are about as trustworthy as beauty salon gossip. There may be truth in it, but who has time to sift it out."

Stella shot me a sideways glance as Mom sliced up the dessert. My much-longed-for snooze was not going to happen. It was time to investigate.

Chapter 29

Secret Touch Strikes Again

Stella was full of anticipation while she and I finished washing Mom's dishes. She kept her voice down but couldn't stop talking about the case.

"If only we could talk to Mrs. Hewitt," she said before shoveling another forkful of pie into her mouth.

"She's still in the hospital," I recalled as I shut the door to the dishwasher and pressed the start button.

Stella eyed the pie. "But her husband isn't. Don't you think he could use a food train?"

"You're volunteering to organize a food train for the Hewitts?" Stella was a great person, but I'd never seen her volunteer to run anything. Sure, she'd sign up and give it her best but organization wasn't her strong point.

"I was thinking we'd jump aboard," Stella said. "Surely someone at the church set something up. We can get Chef Steve to make something amazing and drop it by."

I doubted Mr. Hewitt was far from his wife's side. He probably was sleeping in a painfully straight chair at the hospital. No one would be home to collect our contribution. Still, it would be better for Stella to discover that for herself than to debate it with her.

"I'll call Deacon Brady and see who's in charge," Stella said, ditching me at the sink while I scrubbed the stainless steel.

Steve came along beside me. "Where's she off to?" He asked.

"Just Stella being Stella," I said.

"You mean she's plotting," Steve said. He hoisted himself onto the countertop beside me. His vegan leather gloves flapped from his back pocket. I was glad he hadn't worn them around my parents. It would have stirred up questions.

"Something like that."

Steve cleared his throat, and his voice grew serious. "How are you doing, Corks? Your head and..." Steve waggled his fingers.

I touched the back of my head. The knot was smaller than a dime and no longer tender. "My head is better." It was my turn to flutter my fingers. "This takes some getting used to. I'm not sure if I like or hate it."

"It can't be easy," Steve said,

I smirked. "It's not. Hopefully, I don't have to get used to it." Though as the words came out of my mouth, I cringed. My head was nearly healed, yet my new gift grew stronger.

Steve watched me battle with my own thoughts. "You can handle it, Corky," he said. "You're stronger than you think."

"I second that," Stella said as she walked back into the kitchen with a haughty smirk.

"Uh oh," I said. "It's all you now."

"What does that mean?" Steve asked. Stella sidled up to her brother as he lowered himself to the ground. She gave him puppy dog eyes, along with a side hug. "What does she want?" he asked me.

"She wants you to cook," I said.

"That's nothing new," Steve said. "What do I need to cook and why?"

Three hours after Stella's answer, she and I stood holding a pot of vegetarian chili and skillet cornbread outside the Hewitt's door. The church had a food train set up and was happy to give us the Hewitt's address. I knocked three small raps on the teal door.

Footsteps skittered inside the house. "They must have dogs," Stella said. Snuffling from beyond the door agreed with Stella's hypothesis. Heavier footfalls followed them.

"Calm down, babies," A woman's voice said.

"Is she home already?" I asked.

The face that greeted us wasn't Valerie Hewitt. "Nurse Tunic," I said. My surprise echoed in her eyes as she held back two adorable pups with her legs.

"Miss Hobbs," she said with a smile. "You've sure been busy for someone a week out of the hospital."

"The Hewitts are my favorite clients," I said with honesty.

"We thought we'd join the food train and offer Mr. Hewitt a fresh dinner," Stella said.

Nurse Tunic kneeled to console the sweet guard dogs. She crooked a finger under each one's collars before inviting us in. "Kitchen is on the right."

"Thanks," I said, leading Stella through the foyer.

I leaned in as I set the cornbread on the counter. "How are we supposed to bring up Brandon Daze now?" I whispered to my friend.

She shrugged before opening the fridge and sliding the chili pot into the only empty space. "They're stocked up," she said.

Nurse Tunic rounded the corner to the kitchen seconds after the dogs were sniffing my flip-flops.

"They certainly are," the nurse said. "Henry hasn't been home since the incident. I've been staying here to watch the dogs."

"That's sweet of you," I said as I squatted to pet the dogs. They yipped away before I could get a good scratch in.

"Valerie is my best friend," Nurse Tunic said. "We've been close for years. Emma, her, and I are the three musketeers." She sniffled. "Were."

"I did not know you guys were so close," I said.

Stella rested an elbow on the counter and put her best sympathetic smile on her face. "I figured you worked together but didn't know you were friends."

Nurse Tunic cleared her throat before speaking. "We met through work, but after walking through an ordeal a few years ago, we bonded. The three of us were always on the same page."

"An ordeal?" I asked. "One as bad as Mrs. Hewitt being stalked and threatened?"

"How did you know about that?"

"Mr. Hewitt said something about troubles. Of course, he couldn't tell me any more, but it had to be intense if it bothered Mr. Hewitt."

Nurse Tunic pulled a bar stool over to the kitchen island and settled in. The weight of the traumas orbiting her was obviously wearing her thin. She exhaled before starting her speech. "She'd been threatened for months. At first, we thought it was a disgruntled patient."

"It wasn't?" Stella asked.

I answered. "No, it had to do with a pro-Bono case." Mr. Hewitt's words from our last session came to mind.

"Yeah," Nurse Tunic said. "Free cases come with bonus problems." That was nearly identical to what Mr. Hewitt had said. "This one came with more than its normal share of issues."

"Like what?" Stella asked. I'd filled her in a bit from my mental eavesdropping but wanted to hear the nurse's take on it.

"Threatening letters and phone calls. The feeling of being watched and even having her car keyed," the nurse listed.

"And they all started a couple of months ago?" I asked.

"Yes," the nurse said. "An old client reached out to Valerie. The threats started the next week." My mind immediately went to the Daze family. They must've reached out for help after the death of their son. Maybe his brother had asked the Hewitts for help.

"Because of the client?" Stella asked.

Nurse Tunic shrugged. "It made sense to us, but the police disagreed."

"They knew about the threats?" I asked.

"Of course," Nurse Tunic said. "With our past, we don't mess around with this stuff. If you've lived through a stalker once, you don't want to put up with it again."

"What did the police say?" I asked, hoping they had a better helper than Trent to confide in.

The Nurse rolled her eyes. "Nothing. They believed we were being paranoid."

Stella crossed her arms in distaste. "You talked to Trent, didn't you?"

"Yes," Nurse Tunic said. "He was far from helpful. Valerie and Emma were beside themselves. They were trying to stick it out until Sheriff Austin returned. But none of us thought it would get so dangerous. Now, Valerie's in the hospital, and Emma is dead."

"I know you can't tell us who the client was that brought the drama with them, but can you tell us what triggered the danger last time?" I asked.

Nurse Tunic frowned. "Not that it would do you any good, but it's sure doing my world a lot of harm. No, I'm not dragging you too into it. Least of all you, Miss Hobbs. You've already suffered enough."

Stella gestured with her hands. It was her tell of extreme frustration. Her appearance remained cool, but her hands did all the talking. "That's exactly why we need to know," she argued. "What if the killer comes back to hurt Corky?"

Nurse Tunic frowned as she rose from her seat and pushed away from the countertop. "I think you two should leave." Stella and I followed reluctantly behind the Nurse toward the front door. "It's not safe."

"Thanks for trying to keep us out of it," I said. "But I have one question, was it the Brandon Daze accident?" After asking, I abruptly wrapped the woman in a bear hug and was immediately flooded with the nurse's guilt and fear.

Chapter 30

Brother Suspect

Stella and I sat in my living room twenty minutes later, armed with our favorite frosty beverages and staring at the wall of death.

"Nurse Tunic, Mrs. Hewitt, and Miss Woods were involved in the singles group," Stella said. "And the Brandon Daze incident?"

"Yes," I answered. "Except with Brandon Daze, they were younger. At least in their memory flashes, they were except for Mrs. Hewitt. She's younger in Nurse Tunic's memories but not in her own. Her own thoughts are recent and urgent."

"Too bad Mr. Hewitt wasn't there. I bet he would have answers." Stella tapped her nails along the side of her cup before taking a sip.

"I'm certain he wouldn't spill more than Nurse Tunic," I said. "He's very guarded with client info."

"Good for him," Stella said. "Bad for us."

"Not all bad," I said. "I did catch a little."

"Spill it."

"All three ladies thought they knew who had been with Brandon Daze when he died. If I got the feeling right, they think they know who killed him."

Stella gasped. "So, it wasn't an accident?"

I shook my head. "Not in Nurse Tunic's opinion. She's harboring deep remorse for not bringing his killer to justice."

"Did her flash say who the killer was?" Stella asked.

Again, I shook my head. "Her thoughts continued from guilt and fear to flashes of the Daze family."

Stella leaned forward. "Like Brandon's brother, who was in town for the first time in ten years? Who else would've known the trio from his time here in Deadhorse Canyon?"

I shrugged. "I don't see what silencing the women and pushing for Brandon's justice would do. Wouldn't the family want to see Brandon's killer locked up?"

Stella drummed her fingertips together in a conspiratorial fashion. "Not if you're the one who killed him."

"You think Brandon's brother murdered him?"

Stella held up her index finger. "Give me a moment to work it out. What if, just what if, it was mostly an accident?"

"Mostly?"

"The boys were hanging out, parkouring it or whatever boys do. Brandon slipped and hit his head, and his brother took off to get help?"

I frowned. "Then why didn't help come?"

Stella grimaced. "Perhaps they were too late?"

"They did not find Brandon for hours," I said.

"So," Stella continued her theory. "Brother sees Brandon hit his head. He tries to save him, but it's too late. Then, he's afraid of what people will think, so he heads for the hills. There's nothing he can do anyway, so why take the blame for an accident."

I pursed my lips as I pondered Stella's creative scenario. "I'm not sure I could see a brother close enough to hang out with being that neglectful."

"Unless they really weren't that close, and it was a ruse!"

I blinked at my excitable friend. "What was a ruse? The parkour outing?"

Stella nodded. "Hear me out. Brothers can be a bear. Trust me. I have one. Let's say they had a huge fight, and this outing wasn't something they were supposed to be doing. Brandon's brother takes advantage of an accident to let his adversary die in the fountain."

I sipped my coffee. "I guess it could happen. I don't think Brandon was there alone that night, nor did Nurse Tunic. Someone was there to either watch him die or make it happen."

"Who else do we have?"

I clicked my tongue against my teeth as I thought, then shook my head. "Brandon's brother wasn't at the spa," I said. "That rules him out, remember?"

Stella wagged her index finger at me. "Not necessarily," she said. "We already established the killer had to leave from the backdoor. Perhaps he got in that way as well."

"How would he know he'd find it unlocked? He'd still need inside help," I argued.

I didn't see this brother's past crime angle working. Miss Woods, Mrs. Hewitt, and even Nurse Tunic tried to help the Daze family. They were why the case remained active for as long as it did. From the look of things, they never gave up on it either.

Stella scrolled through her phone. Her eyes flickered across the screen. "I've made up my mind," she said, without looking up. "I'm stalking the guy."

"What?" A chortle slipped from my lips. "You can't," I said, once I realized she was serious. "What if he comes after you?"

Stella waved her hand at me. "I'm nobody to him. You, however, you're an eyewitness. I'll be careful."

I frowned. Stella's avoidance of eye contact was a telltale sign. She was going ahead with her disastrous plan no matter what I said. I scrambled for an excuse to keep her in my living room. My doubts about Brandon's brother being a murderer were solid, but that didn't mean they were flawless. Maybe Stella saw something there that I couldn't. If so, how could I let her place herself in harm's way?

A piteous reason for her to stay formed. "What if Mel calls?"

"About what?" Stella snorted.

"Clean up," I spat. "We both need the extra funds." Stella put her hands on her hips and frowned. For a quick second, I thought I'd snagged her until Stella picked up her purse and pulled out her keys.

"Call me," she said. "I'll meet you there." Stella didn't look backward as she speed-walked from my cottage. I stared after her and prayed that she'd stay safe. I shot a text to Steve to alert him.

"Stella's on the move."

"What's new?"

"She's following a suspect."

"Who?" I filled in the blanks and was greeted by a "meh" emoji. "I'll walk over and check on her."

I sank onto my couch with a hefty sigh before sipping the last of my coffee and tossed my phone on the hospital's plastic bag. Meanwhile, the crime scene stared down at me.

Something wasn't sitting right. Stella was determined to hunt down the killer and get life back to normal. I admired her tenacity but couldn't shake the feeling that she was headed in the wrong direction. However, what other suspects did we have? Did I need to rub up against everyone in town to get a hit on the killer? I shuddered. What a horrible thought.

I held up one hand, admiring it and the new power hidden beneath the skin. My ability wasn't waning, even though my head barely ached anymore. Was this strange talent sticking around for good? If so, I'd have to do more testing. Pleather gloves and hiding from hugs would not save me forever. Though my secret sifting had come in handy with Nurse Tunic, the woman held more secrets than I could sponge. However, if I wanted to know more, I'd have to lead the conversation to a topic I wanted to investigate. Could I do that all the time? Or would someone's loudest thoughts come out whether I beckoned them or not?

A sudden urge to journal overtook me. I launched from the couch and hustled to my room. Right when I was about to put a purple pen to paper, my phone chirped from the coffee table.

"Stella," I groaned.

Stubbing my toe on the door jamb, I hurried to my phone, certain it was my invasive best friend. Sure enough, her message sat waiting for acknowledgment.

"Brandon's brother is a locksmith!" The text caught me unaware. Then came the picture of the van parked in the Daze driveway. "Access explained."

Stella was right.

Chapter 31
The Lost Earbud

My phone buzzed in my hand, startling me out of my skin. A text from Davis read, "Mel moved cleaning day to now. Are you coming?"

I shuddered. Cleaning up a crime scene wasn't on my dream come true list, especially since I'd been part of the scene. However, Stella needed the cash, and I couldn't let Mel slip this opportunity past her.

I replied with a thumbs up and spread the news to Stella, who took it just as I figured she would.

"Why didn't she text us?" Her message read.

I answered with an eye roll GIF.

"I'll meet you there soon. Steve needs the truck. He'll drop me."

I replied with a smiley face, though I felt far from jolly. Trekking to the spa wouldn't be too bad. The weather had cooled as the sky hinted at an oncoming summer storm. If I hustled, I'd make it to Hands-On before thunder cracked loose the rain. I grabbed my gloves and shoved them in the pockets of my cotton hoodie before tying it around my waist. Preparedness was always better than not. I then locked my cottage door and walked down the sidewalk.

Davis paced in front of the spa as I strolled up. He was on edge, probably because Melinda wasn't there yet. It was just like her to send an all-out alert and then to be late. To make things even more frustrating, the summer sky drizzled. I pulled on my hoodie top and stepped under the Hands-On awning.

"Mel's late," I said stupidly.

"What's new?" Davis answered. His voice trembled slightly. He was even more agitated than I'd guessed. "Bullies can't be trusted."

I nodded, remembering my talk with Davis the day of the attack. He was always encouraging me to stand up to Melinda.

"Where's your other half?" Davis asked as he scanned the street.

"Stella's running an errand," I said. Davis didn't need to know she was stalking down a suspect.

"That girl knows how to find trouble, doesn't she?"

I rolled my eyes. "You don't know half of it."

Davis dug his hands into his jacket's pockets. His windbreaker repelled the falling rain, whereas my cotton soaked in the drips. "Then again," he said. "You walked in on a murder and not her."

I shivered. "Don't remind me. I can't help replaying that night over and over."

"Being back at the scene can't help," Davis said.

"It doesn't," I answered. "It brings back all the feels."

"What about the memories? Do you see those more clearly?" Davis asked. I paused, thinking it over.

"Not yet," I said. "But I'm hopeful." I offered Davis a half-hearted smile.

He was conversing politely, but I didn't want to mull over the crime at the moment. It was hard enough to think about in the safety of my living room. Being a wall away from where I'd been attacked gave me an eerie sense of foreboding. I stepped closer to Davis, wishing Stella and Steve would hurry.

"Be careful what you wish for," Davis said as if reading my thoughts. Except he wasn't referring to my late friend. He pivoted back to crime. "What do you remember about that night?"

I frowned at him before I could correct my overly expressive face. "Not much," I said.

"Smells? Sounds? Faces?"

I shook my head, trying to think of another way to detour Davis's line of questions. He pulled his cell from his pocket. "It's Mel," he said. "She says to let ourselves in."

"That would be great," I whined. "If we had a key."

Davis lifted a small bundle of keys from his jacket pocket. They snagged on his jeans, sending a small projectile flying from their ring. "I have the backup set. For when I have to open."

He turned to the front door. The keys jangled as he unlocked the main entrance. I stepped closer to the door and nearly stepped on something. A small sparkle caught my eye.

"You dropped this," I said, kneeling to collect the tiny object. I scooped it into my hand without a thought, and then carefully observed it. The rose gold companion ear bud to Miss Woods's shimmered up at me. My hand shook uncontrollably.

I flashed backward in time. It had been raining the day of my attack. Davis was wearing the same coat as that day. But it couldn't be Davis, I thought. He was too sweet and kind. An encouragement to his core, he kept the spa customers smiling and safe. He'd even lifted me up whenever Melinda strove to slap me down. But if he wasn't the killer, why did he have Miss's Woods earbud in his pocket?

I felt Davis's shadow loom above me. My brain stuttered as it pieced things together.

Davis grabbed my hoodie and tugged me into the spa, using my hood as a handle. He slammed the door behind us and tossed me onto the hardwood entryway. I skittered away like a crab, dropping Miss Woods's earbud. It clanked away across the floor, ticking like a time bomb. How had Davis not made my list? He'd been there- the entire time.

 "Why would you kill Miss Woods?" I asked before my courage left me.

 Davis's face fell. His expression was one of genuine confusion and loneliness. "Oh, Corky, where should I start?"

 He sank to the floor and sat with his back leaning against the front door. I blinked at him. How could he be so casual about killing someone? Unless he'd done it before and gotten away with it?

 "Brandon Daze," I whispered.

Davis grinned. "I knew you'd understand," he said. Again, I blinked at him and searched for a weapon in my peripherals. "We talked about it, remember?" I shook my head. Davis frowned. "Bullies. I told you I finally stuck it to mine. Beat him at his own game."

"You killed Brandon? In high school?"

"Some people just don't know when to quit," Davis said. I backed up a smidgen. He scowled. "Like you, right now. Stop that, or I'll take your actions personally."

I paused as my heart rate ramped up. It wasn't like Davis had another way out. He had to silence me if he hoped to escape.

"Miss Woods knew you killed him?" I asked, already knowing the answer.

"Counselors," Davis spat. "They think they know everything. She made my parents send me to a shrink because of Brandon's bullying. I never lived that down. They taunted me about being crazy from the very beginning of therapy."

"The Hewitts?" I asked, piecing things together a little at a time.

Davis sniffled. He swiped at baby tears forming in his eyes. I wanted the scoop, but more than that, I needed proof to get the police to look at Davis. "They all suspected you," I said.

Davis sniffled. "Always."

"So why move back to town?"

Davis snorted. "I figured they'd be gone. This is home, after all, and I wanted to come home."

My stomach recoiled. Davis had snapped long ago. Before we'd met. I didn't have time to think about it. Now

I had to find some way to distract him, so I could escape with my life. Just then, a loud pop resounded from outside.

"God bless you, Stella Michaels," I thought, thrilled that my bestie drove an old clunker. Davis flinched and stood up, staring out the front door. I launched to my feet and charged down the back hallway.

"No!" Davis fumbled behind me. I was fast, but his strides were much larger than mine. He grabbed the back of my jacket as my fingers brushed the back door handle.

I fell face-first against the door, slamming my forehead against the jamb. When my knees hit the carpet, I could hear the front door open. "It's Davis!" I shouted as loud as I could, once air returned to my lungs. "Call for help!"

"No!" Davis grabbed the back of my neck.

As his skin hit mine, memories of his treacherous deeds overwhelmed me. Luring Brandon to the fountain and holding him under were moments of pride for Davis. The memory of Miss Woods recognizing Davis in the hall of Hands-On sent ripples of terror through my stomach, followed by a snicker of plotting. No remorse tainted Davis's recall. I was about to get sick when Davis flipped me over to face him, but it wasn't his face I spotted first. It was Steve's.

Already upon Davis, Steve pulled my murderous coworker from on top of me and shoved him into the nearest treatment room. I pushed up on my elbows, too stunned to do much else. Stella raced down the hall from reception and came to my aid.

Steve reappeared with a red welt forming on his cheek. I reached out to touch the heroic injury, only to have him stop me with a gloved hand.

"Thanks for remembering," I whispered.

Steve grinned softly. Stella crushed me into a group hug with Steve. Stella's brown noise buzz drowned thoughts of Steve and me sitting on a porch swing watching two dark-haired kiddos chase ladybugs. I lounged in the presence of my friends after catching a glance of Davis knocked out under a treatment table. Trent arrived moments later with backup.

Chapter 32

Time for Corky

The spa sat vacant a week later, awaiting professional cleaners and designers. The owner shut everything down to give the spa a complete overhaul. Meanwhile, Stella and I were out of a job. Well, I was.

While working part-time at Belly Up Burgers, Stella wrangled a few facials from her regulars. It wasn't ideal. I couldn't imagine returning to the same space where someone had attacked me twice. I prayed the makeover would be enough to put my heart at ease and allow me to carry on with business as usual. However, my special superpower hadn't left yet. Maybe once the spa reopened, I'd also have a handle on that.

For the moment, I took each day as it came and journaled my way through two brand-new notebooks. Mrs. Hewitt met with me over the Internet to chat, but she wasn't ready for in-person therapy yet. I didn't blame her. If anyone understood how she felt, it was me.

After the police carted Davis away, I returned home with a new resolve. I flipped open my laptop and deleted my old email account. No one but Brett emailed me there, and now he couldn't reach me that way either. A weight lifted as I created a new address for new friends and clients. Melinda could have Brett one hundred percent to herself. I was done. It was time to start again.

Time to be Corky, whoever that might be, without strings or guilt attached.

It was also time to start closure. Standing between Steve and Stella, I cried over Miss Woods's gravesite. It was time to say goodbye and ask her to forgive me. Perhaps I could've saved her from her watery fate if I'd been faster or more aware. I hadn't spoken that thought aloud. But my journals had heard about it. As long as I kept Stella out of the pages, it was a secret I'd hold on to for now.

I bent and dropped the rouge earbud onto the headstone marker. It was a cheesy thing to do, but it eased my heart to do it. When I rose, both of my friends took hold of my hands. Stella's bare skin sent buzzes through my head, and

Steve's gloved hand released no new secrets.

However, when I cried unexpectedly at Brandon Daze's gravesite, Steve floundered for a moment before wrapping me in a brotherly hug. I nuzzled against him, my cheek brushing his neck as I wept.

A slurry of feeling overtook me as Steve lifted my chin in his hand and kissed my tears away. I pulled away, blinking. Tears clouded my vision, but I could sense the awkwardness growing between Steve and me. It took a moment for me to realize the kisses hadn't been real. They'd been secret thoughts of my best friend's brother. I deflated. What in the world was going on?

Stella bumbled halfway up the hill and hollered, "Come on! Let's grab a coffee!"

Steve blinked at me. "You alright, Corks?" he asked. His eyes searched mine for reassurance.

I smiled, unsure if I could pull off casual after the sentimental secret flash. "I will be," I answered.

"I know you will," Steve said. He took my hand in his and squeezed it before releasing me. It was a gesture he'd done thousands of times before. Somehow it meant something sweeter now. "We believe in you, Corky Hobbs."

"I know," I whispered. Now it was my turn to believe in me too.

Corky's next mystery will be out soon and will reveal even more about your favorite superhero masseuse. Filled with secrets, snark, and a new furry friend- Under Acupressure will knock your socks off.

In the meantime, get a sneak peek at Sarah's two other mystery series.

Sign up for her newsletter so you don't miss a single clue.

https://storyoriginapp.com/giveaways/f3beb852-9031-11ed-b4b8-0f25ae2c32fd

Or visit her website to learn more.

www.sarahhualde.com

Made in the USA
Monee, IL
19 March 2026

46346168R00194